JEREMIAH'S PROMISE

Jeremiah's Promise

An Adventure in Modern Israel

Kenneth D. Roseman, Ph.D.

UAHC Press
New York

Dedicated to the early settlers of the Yishuv, who left home and hearth for an unknown land where they could pursue vision and dreams—today's Eretz Yisrael is their gift to us and our children.

Acknowledgements

Many thanks to Rabbi Hara Person and her devoted colleagues at the UAHC Press, Ken Gesser, Stuart Benick, who continually encouraged, prodded and cajoled me in the completion and improvement of this book, and to Rick Abrams, Liane Broido, Debra Hirsch Corman, Rachel Gleiberman, and Benjamin David, who each did their part to bring this book forth.

Maps by May Swab, Mapping Specialists Limited.

Library of Congress Cataloging-in-Publication Data

Roseman, Kenneth.
    Jeremiah's promise : an adventure in modern Israel / Kenneth D. Roseman.
    p. cm. -- (The do-it-yourself adventure series / by Kenneth D. Roseman)
    Summary: As a young Jewish survivor of the Holocaust in Poland who emigrates to Palestine in 1945 and lives in the new state of Israel, the reader makes choices which affect his family, his residence, his career, his country, and his sense of identity as a Jew.
    ISBN 0-8074-0787-9 (pbk. : alk. paper)
    1. Jews--Israel--Juvenile fiction. 2. Israel--History--20th century--Juvenile fiction. 3. Plot-your-own stories. [1. Jews--Israel--Fiction. 2. Israel--History--20th century--Fiction. 3. Conduct of life--Fiction. 4. Holocaust survivors--Fiction. 5. Palestine--History--20th century--Fiction. 6. Plot-your-own stories.] I. Title.

PZ7.R71863 Je 2002
[Fic]--dc21

2002017994

My dear young friends:

When I was much younger, probably just about your age, I loved to pretend that I was someone else. I could use my imagination to live anywhere in the world at any time in history. Trying to think like another person stretched my mind in many ways, but most of all it was fun. I really enjoyed the world of my imagination (and it wouldn't surprise me at all if you do, too!), although I always knew that I was actually myself.

Later on, I experimented a little bit with acting in plays. When I put on a costume and took the role of some character, again I could imagine what that person must have been like. When I became an adult, I studied history so that I could truly find out what people (especially Jewish people) were like from the time of the Bible until today. Now, I write books for you and your friends so that you can use your imaginations in the same way and become a participant in and creator of the drama that we call Jewish history.

This book is a little different from the six other ones I have written. Those were all about people who are no longer alive. Some of them died a very long time ago; some of them died more recently. But all of them are dead. The characters in this book are still alive today, because this book is about the country called Israel, which has only been a nation since 1948.

Many Jews have relatives and friends in Israel. If you do—or if you know someone who does—you could write or e-mail back and forth to discuss what you read about in this book. I hope you will someday have the opportunity to visit Israel and see the places that this book talks about. You see, the events, the places, and the people in this book are real. Of course, no one person could have had all the experiences about which you're going to read. But I didn't have to make anything up. All I did was combine real adventures into the lives of one family so that you could think about the problems and the choices they faced—and still face.

So, this is a book about real people, people who are not so different from you. The choices and decisions they make are interesting and, sometimes, difficult. You'll have the opportunity to make the same choices as you read, and maybe that will help you understand them better.

When you have to make a choice to move the story ahead, think about what makes one choice better than the other. The reasons we go one way rather than another are called "values." We use them every day, and so do the people in this book. Ask yourself: What values would the people in this book use to make their choices? Are their values the same as yours? If they are not, what makes them different?

But, remember, people are pretty much the same, wherever they live. They want the same things that we want (security, hope, love, food, shelter, a sense of importance, etc.), and they make their choices to secure these goals.

When you get to the end of one story, try going back and taking a different path. You may be surprised to find out how other choices affect the outcome. Human choice does make a lot of difference in how history turns out. We are not robots, just acting in a play written by someone else. We are people who make decisions, sometimes for good reasons and sometimes not, and our choices really do count.

Most of all, I hope you have a great deal of fun and excitement as you make your choices and build the modern State of Israel.

Kenneth D. Roseman, Ph.D.
Senior Rabbi, Temple Shalom
Dallas, Texas

Legend:
All words in **bold** can be found on a map or in the glossary.

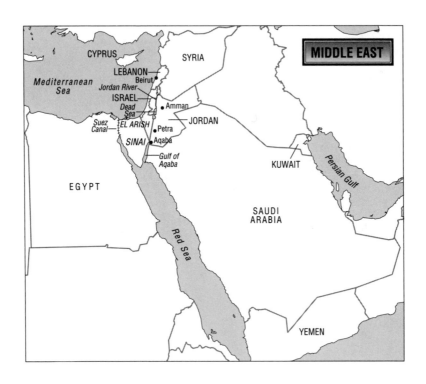

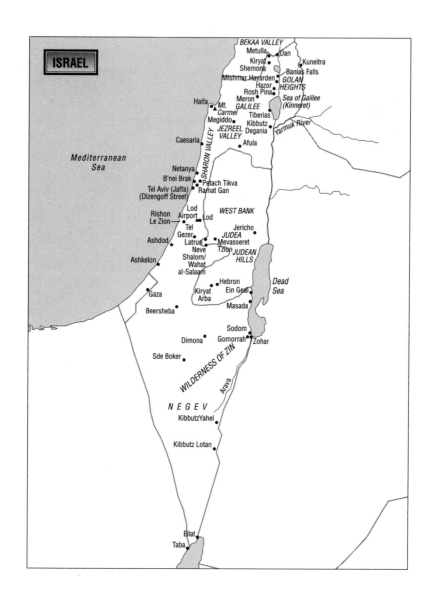

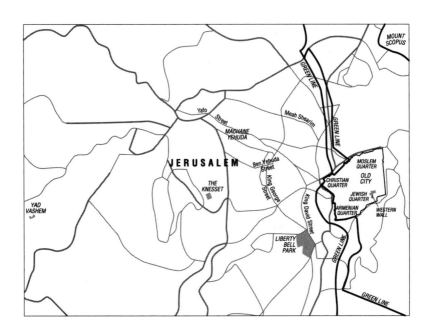

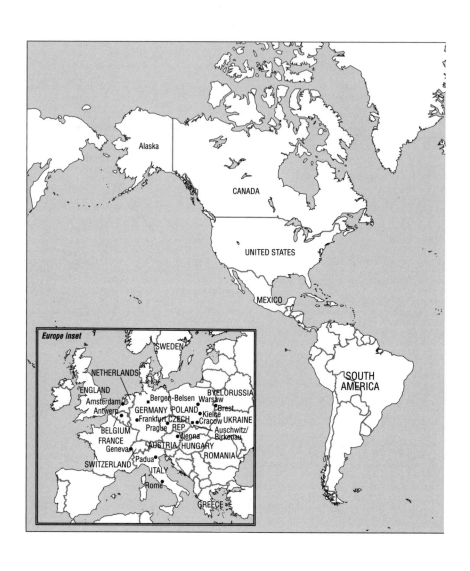

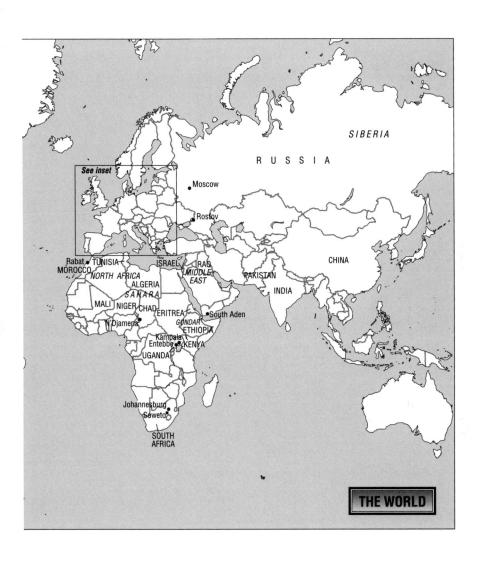

SIBERIA

R U S S I A

See inset

Moscow

Rostov

CHINA

Rabat TUNISIA
MOROCCO
NORTH AFRICA
ALGERIA
SAHARA
MALI NIGER CHAD
N'Djamena
ISRAEL IRAQ
MIDDLE
EAST
PAKISTAN
INDIA
ERITREA
GONDAR South Aden
ETHIOPIA
Kampala
Entebbe KENYA
UGANDA

Johannesburg
Soweto

SOUTH
AFRICA

THE WORLD

I had God's word: Hanamel, the son of your uncle Shallum, will come to you and say: "Purchase my field in Anathoth because yours is the kinsman's right."

I bought the field . . . and I took the deed of purchase (the sealed one . . . together with the open one) and gave the deed to Baruch. . . in the presence of Hanamel . . . and the witnesses who signed the deed [and] in the presence of all the Judeans in the court of the guard, and charged Baruch before them . . . : "Take these deeds, the sealed one and the open one, and put them in an earthen jar, that they may last for many days."

For so the Lord of Hosts, Israel's God, has said: "Fields and vineyards shall yet be purchased in this land."

Jeremiah 32:6–15 (selections)
Translation from Sheldon Blank,
Jeremiah: Man and Prophet

1

As the spring of 1945 became a warmer summer, hope grew in your spirit. The horrors of World War II were now ended; the dreaded German **Nazis** had been defeated; you had survived. The terrors of three years in the concentration camps of **Bergen-Belsen** and **Birkenau** and **Auschwitz** would never be erased from your memory. You doubted that you would ever see any of your family again. Most of **Poland**'s 3,500,000 Jews had been murdered by the invaders, and those few who, like you, had survived, were scattered to the four winds. Still, there is hope for the future. It is time to go home.

You were a tall and muscular man before the war, but now the starvation, forced labor, and tortures of the camps have left you but a shadow of your former self. Nearly six feet tall, you weigh only eighty-five pounds, and you can hardly summon up the energy to walk from your wooden bunk to the ambulance that waits for you outside the barracks of the concentration camp. It will take you to a hospital where, slowly, you will gain weight and strength.

For a year, you follow the doctors' orders of diet and exercise, gradually becoming more like your pre-war self. Finally, in June of 1946, you leave the hospital. A Russian army truck takes you north to your hometown of **Kielce**, halfway between **Cracow** and **Warsaw**. There, you hope to find some other survivors like yourself, Jews who are struggling to resume the life they had known before the *Shoah*. But you are met in **Kielce** by a terrifying surprise.

2

A story has been circulated that sixteen Christian children had been kidnapped by Jews and all but one of them murdered. Though this tale eventually is proved to be a falsehood, many local Poles believe it. A mob gathers and turns on the Jews who have returned to **Kielce** after the horrors of the Holocaust. Forty-one Jews are slaughtered, and many more are injured. It seems unbelievable that even though the Holocaust is over, Jews are still being killed in Europe. Yet it is all too true. Your former neighbors and friends have turned against you, and even the Catholic Church seems to approve of the massacre. As time goes on, you hear of similar stories from other Polish cities. First, the **Nazis** murdered most of **Poland**'s Jews; now, the few survivors are being set upon, even killed, by the people of the towns to which they have returned.

Quickly, you reach a decision. **Poland** can no longer be your home; the anti-Semites have made that very clear, and you have understood their message. **Kielce** may have been your home before the war, but it is no longer the same city you once knew. The only choice you have is to take to the road again, to flee to the west and seek a new life in some more hospitable place.

Along with thousands of like-minded Polish Jews, you hitchhike on passing trucks, jump on freight trains, trek through forests and fields, often sleeping in the open at night. Fortunately, the weather is mild during the long days of summer, and you are finally able to reach the **displaced persons' camp** at Zeilsheim near **Frankfurt** in western **Germany**.

3

Conditions in the camp are difficult. There had hardly been enough space for the tens of thousands of refugees who had arrived before you; now, another sixty thousand Jews have fled **Poland** in three months, and many of them crowd into the Zeilsheim camp. After seven hundred miles of difficult travel, all of you are hungry and tired. Some of you are ill, and none of you have much money or any more clothing than you can carry on your back. Representatives from the United States Army, the American Jewish Joint Distribution Committee, and the United Nations Relief and Rehabilitation Commission (UNRRA), as well as several Jewish groups from Palestine, work desperately to provide food, shelter, health care, and other necessities for you.

But you understand something right away. This is not a place where you will be able to stay for any length of time. Zeilsheim is only going to be a temporary home for you until you find a better place.

During the reading of the *M'gillah* on Purim in 1947, an agent of the Mossad L'Aliyah Bet, a secret group helping Jews get to Palestine, starts a conversation with you. "I've noticed," he says, "that you are stronger than many other people here. You are the kind of immigrant the *yishuv* in Palestine can use. I believe we can smuggle you into Palestine illegally. There's some chance that you will be arrested by the British, but there is also a good chance you'll be able to sneak in and settle in the Jewish homeland. Don't you think it's worth a try; anything would be better than staying here!"

You've got to think about this offer, and there is no better place to think than sitting alone in the camp's makeshift synagogue. As you fidget on the hard bench, you thumb through a copy of the *Tanach,* and your fingers turn the pages, as if by intent, to the thirty-second chapter of **Jeremiah**. Just before he left **Eretz Yisrael**, you read, the **prophet** bought a plot of ground, sealed the deed in a clay jar, and buried it. This was his promise to future generations of Jews: they would always have the right of ownership to this sacred place.

4

Nothing could be clearer. This Jewish Palestinian is right. **Jeremiah**'s promise applies to you; you have a right to the Land of Israel. It's been your possession since biblical times. Even if you could not live there, the buried deed affirms that it is yours. Besides, anything would be better than simply hanging around this **displaced persons' camp** until someone else decided what you are to do. It's time to make some decisions and to take charge of your own future.

With forged papers that identify you as an Italian Jew returning to his home near **Rome**, you hop in the back of an American army truck. The driver is an American military chaplain, **Rabbi Eugene Lipman**. The trip is against his orders, but saving Jewish lives is his highest goal, even if it means he will get into trouble.

But there is no trouble. You pass across the border and enter **Italy** with no difficulty. For a few days, you stay in a **Jewish Brigade** camp near **Padua**. Then you continue to a **kibbutz**-type settlement at **Nonantola**, where hundreds of refugees like yourself are preparing for a new life in Palestine.

Finally, a message is passed to you: the ship is ready. Tomorrow night, you will sail toward **Haifa** and, you hope, a life of freedom in a Jewish land. The ship is called *Exodus,* a very old and tired ship. It travels slowly, but steadily, eastward past **Greece**, nearer and nearer to Palestine. At night, not a single light is allowed on the ship, because the British navy is on the lookout for ships just like this one, full of illegal immigrants.

As the sun rises, you can finally see the coastline of Palestine and the hills of **Haifa**. But you can also see a British frigate sailing just a few hundred yards off *Exodus*'s starboard side. They will surely try to stop you from entering the "Promised Land."

If you believe that you can succeed in outrunning the British blockade, turn to page 163.

If, however, your illegal attempt to enter the Land fails, turn to page 112.

5

As you sit on the veranda of your little bungalow, the manager of **Yahel**'s greenhouse approaches you. He looks worried, and you ask him if there is anything you can do to help. "My friend," he says, slumping down into a chair, "we're in trouble, deep trouble. I've got to have fresh water to grow our flowers. Without the flowers to sell, the **kibbutz** doesn't have any money. But there doesn't seem to be enough water. The pressure in the system is dropping every day; soon, the hoses will just spray out air.

"Besides, we're having to pay a lot more for our electricity. All the pumps we use to draw water run on electricity, so that means that we are using more and more of our resources to water the flowers—with water that we may not even have. *Oy vey*, are we in trouble!"

He's right, of course. Without these two vital commodities, water and power, the entire region of the **Negev**, far more than just **Kibbutz Yahel**, is at risk. If these supplies fail or if you cannot afford to buy them, you cannot live in this area. But you think there is a way to address these concerns.

You persuade the leaders of the **kibbutz** to hire a team of scientists from both the **Technion** in **Haifa** and the **Weizmann Institute of Science** in **Ramat Gan**. These scholars are used to working together on problems, and they meet you with excitement and enthusiasm. "How can we make it possible for the desert to bloom?" you ask them.

One group focuses its efforts on the issue of water. You can work with them on page 113.

The other group thinks about electrical power on page 114.

6

Y ou realize that you could irrigate a few acres, perhaps a hundred, and keep the crops growing with sprinklers and hoses and a steady flow of water. But water is scarce and expensive, and if you are ever to do anything to help the people in **sub-Saharan Africa**, for sure you cannot develop a technique that uses so much water. They simply don't have it!

But the agronomists in **Jericho** have had a brainstorm. "What's the point," they ask, "of watering the ground in between the plants? Nothing is going to grow in that soil. We need to concentrate our precious water right on the fragile plant itself. That's the only place where we should use this resource."

They have laid out a little black tube along each row of plants. At exactly the place where the stem of the plant goes into the ground, they have pierced a tiny hole in the tube, a hole just big enough to let a drop of water escape from this network of tiny hoses. Drip, drip, drip. The water flows out precisely where it is needed, and only there; nothing is wasted in between the plants.

What a great idea! What is it called? Drip irrigation. It conserves a precious and expensive resource and still lets the vegetables grow. This is a technique you can use in **Sodom**, and it is a method you can export around the world. You are really getting somewhere now.

*If you spend the rest of your life perfecting this system in your test plots near **Sodom**, turn to page 60.*

If you cannot wait to share this method with others, turn to page 51.

7

There is a long period of silence. The rabbis are thinking. Perhaps they are looking up something in one of their law books. Or, perhaps, they are praying. Then you hear a voice. It can only be the voice of the chief judge of the rabbinical council. He speaks slowly: "*Pikuach nefesh,* saving a life, must always come first. If we have to choose between these two values, both of which are good, we shall always decide in favor of life. Doctors, you may use these kidneys to save the lives of two other people. That is not a violation of the **halachah**. In fact, it is in keeping with the highest principles of Judaism and Jewish law.

"And," he continues, "we have concluded that you must use your best medical judgment about who is to receive the kidneys. If the girl from **Hebron** is the best candidate for transplant in your professional judgment, then she should be the one. After all, who are we to decide between one human being and another? All people are equally created in God's image, whether they are Jews or **Moslems**, Israelis or Palestinians. That is our decision. Now go, and do what you must do."

You sigh a deep sigh of relief. This has been Jewish law solving a problem at its finest and highest level. This is Jewish ethics at work. You are very proud to have been a witness to this moment. "*L'chayim,*" you say quietly, "to life. May Judaism always be a religion that chooses life."

END

8

There are two main political parties in the **Knesset**, the Labor Party on the liberal or left side and the Likud Party, which is more conservative. Yes, it is true that a Likud prime minister, **Menachem Begin**, was the one who worked out a peace treaty with the Egyptians, but most of what you know about that party makes you doubt whether they will lead Israel toward *shalom*.

So you join the party of **Yitzchak Rabin** and **Shimon Peres**, and you work very hard. For a long time, you get little recognition for the door-to-door campaigning that you do in various neighborhoods. Finally, however, you are rewarded by a place on the Labor Party list of candidates for the 120 seats in the **Knesset**. The election sweeps your party into office, and **Rabin** gives you a seat on the committee that will continue the negotiations with the Palestinians. What better position could you have if you want to influence the search for peace!

After some frustrating meetings, you learn that the president of the **United States**, Bill Clinton, has asked both Prime Minister **Rabin** and **PLO** Chairman **Yasir Arafat** to come to **Washington, D.C.** He is convinced that face-to-face discussions will move the peace process forward. And, indeed, they do.

On a beautiful sunny afternoon, you stand off to the side as these three world leaders gather on the lawn of the White House. It's a scene you never thought you would ever witness— Palestinians, Israelis, and Americans all shaking hands. You do not know whether this peace agreement will last. Maybe it won't. But any peace seems better to you than war and killing. *Shalom* is and will be your most important goal.

END

9

One **Shabbat** afternoon, you walk down to the dig with your daughter and her own little son, your grandson. As you look at the excavated ruins of the ancient world, you think about your own life, where you started, the road you traveled to reach this place, all the many things that have happened to you in between. Many years and many miles, but here you stand, three generations of a family, looking now at history that goes back, perhaps, thirty generations.

Your eyes are pulled steadily, inescapably toward the layer of gray ash . . . the burned residue of the **Second Temple.** Since it was destroyed, Jews have been scattered all across the globe. This people has lived everywhere, under almost every circumstance imaginable. Empires have tried to destroy the Jewish people, yet here you are. Here all three of you are, right back where it all began, right back at the center of the Jewish world, right back at the center of that center, the Temple in the middle of **Jerusalem.**

You think of the miracle of Jewish survival, of your own personal survival . . . and how your people has begun life again in a new land. You curl your arm around your daughter's shoulder. "We began here. And here we begin again. Every day we make our history come alive. Thank God for the miracle of the Jewish people!"

END

10

As you think about how this new law should read, you realize that there is a problem. Various groups within the Jewish world understand "conversion" in different ways. And it is not at all clear that a conversion ceremony conducted by a **Reform** Jewish rabbi will be the same as one conducted by a Conservative or **Orthodox** rabbi. Each one will think that the ceremony of that group of Jews is right and appropriate. But an **Orthodox** rabbi will not accept as valid the conversions performed by others.

You set up a meeting with the leadership of the National Religious Party, Israel's most powerful **Orthodox** political group. "We don't want this issue to tear our brand-new country apart," you tell them. "The issue is not tearing Israel apart," they respond. "It's those other rabbis and other movements who refuse to follow Jewish law. If only they would behave according to the **halachah**, we would have no problem."

Yet even these very **Orthodox** rabbis understand the concept of compromise. "Perhaps," you suggest, "we can work it out this way. Suppose that we agree that any conversion done in Israel must be performed according to your standards, by rabbis who are acceptable to you. But would you accept the idea that any conversion done elsewhere, so long as it is performed by a recognized Jewish movement, would be accepted by Israeli law? Would that be fair?" They aren't very happy with this arrangement, but as Prime Minister **David Ben-Gurion** insists on the arrangement, they really have no choice. "We still want all conversions to be done according to *halachah*, according to traditional Jewish law. We may be willing to go along with you now, but you can be sure that we'll fight for what we believe in the future."

Your interest in this controversy continues. Turn to page 57.

11

"Let everyone who is hungry come and eat." This line sticks in your mind, even after the Passover seder is over. You recline in your living room, so full of food that you are actually uncomfortable, but you cannot eliminate the vision of so many people in the world who cannot come to eat, who do not have enough food, whose children have bloated bellies and spindly arms. Now that you have conquered hunger for your own family, you feel compelled to do something for at least some of these other people.

Maimonides taught that the highest form of charity is to teach others how to take care of themselves. If you could act on this principle and make this advice come to life, wouldn't you be doing so much more for the starving people of the world than if you simply sent them a little food! If they could only learn how to grow their own crops more effectively, they might never again need help from you or anyone else.

You are particularly moved by the plight of people in the area of **Africa** south of the **Sahara Desert.** There is little rainfall in this region, and recently a famine has raged through these countries. More than anyone in virtually any other area of the world, these pitiful men, women, and children desperately need your help. But you are not sure what you can do. After all, you are only one person, and this is an immense region with many tribes of native peoples and many different problems.

One possibility is to experiment with a system that makes efficient use of a little water. If you think that you can do something by perfecting this technique and then sharing it, turn to page 151.

If, on the other hand, you do not feel that you can wait for the experiment to develop because people are dying right now, turn to page 21.

12

After what you saw and experienced in the concentration camps during World War II, how can you believe in God? Religion could not save your family from the death camps of the **Nazis**. Even in the short time that you have been in Palestine, you have seen constant quarreling between different religious sects. **Chasidic** Jews cannot agree with each other or with other **Orthodox** Jews; religious Jews and nonreligious Jews cannot seem to get along; **Socialist** Jews argue with just about everyone.

You had imagined that after Jews died just because they were Jewish, regardless of what they believed or did not believe, that all Jews would have a common bond. Would it not make sense that the rebuilding of the Jewish people would silence the petty disagreements and that all Jews would be able to get along with each other?

You have heard about **kibbutzim**, but not a lot. In your *shtetl* in **Poland**, no one talked about **Zionism** or **socialism**, and the new kinds of communities being created in Palestine were far from anyone's attention. It was enough simply to worry about surviving another day and having enough food for the family.

But now, here in Israel, you learn about the **kibbutz**. No one there owns any property; everything belongs to the group. Each member of the community has only what is needed for a good life. To be sure, there are debates about how the money and houses and other goods will be divided, but the discussions always end up with agreement. Perhaps it is on the **kibbutz** that you will finally find Jews agreeing.

*If you decide to try living on a **kibbutz**, turn to page 26.*

If another style of collective life appeals to you more, turn to page 35.

13

The newspapers and the television have told you that something big will be happening today. At noon, you and your daughter and her brand-new son are glued to the television set as pictures of Ben-Gurion Airport flicker on the screen. Then an EgyptAir jet plane pulls up to a red carpet, and a tall man walks down the steps. Who would ever have believed that **Anwar Sadat,** president of **Egypt,** would be shaking hands with Prime Minister **Menachem Begin** on Israeli soil! **Sadat** tells the audience that he is ready to take any risk in the pursuit of peace.

You turn to your daughter. "I have fought these Arabs in several wars. I know how they think. You cannot trust them at all. I would never make peace, even if **Sadat** himself came into this very living room!"

Your daughter turns to you with tears in her eyes. "*Abba,* I know what you have been through. But times have changed. There is a lot of Israeli blood that has been spilled in the **Sinai.** Now, I have a son and you have a grandson. Isn't peace worth a chance? Maybe his blood will never have to be mixed into those burning sands. Enough death has happened. Let's see if we can't stop the killing."

You're not sure that she is right. But if you are willing to give her perspective a try, turn to page 87.

If something happens that you believe proves you right, turn to page 174.

14

Military life has been good for you. You know you are contributing to the safety of the new nation, and you are proud of yourself as a Jew. No one will ever accuse you of surrendering passively to your people's enemies.

But Israel is a tiny country. In this new age of tanks and artillery cannons that can shoot twenty or so miles and fast airplanes, Israel cannot rely only on foot soldiers. You are convinced that a powerful air force is absolutely necessary for the defense of the country. So, you and seven other officers (two of them women!) travel to the **United States** to learn more about aircraft, how they are built and how they are flown in combat.

Some of you have a more technical interest, and this group goes to the Boeing Aircraft factory near **Seattle, Washington**. The rest of you end up at Randolph Air Force Base in **San Antonio, Texas**, where you take flight training. After six months, all of you graduate; you are very proud to be the first five pilots of the new Israeli air force—and even prouder that one of your colleagues is the first woman pilot.

While you are in **Texas**, you meet a wonderful young Jewish woman, and you fall in love. After you marry, she asks you a difficult question. Are you determined to move back to Israel, or will you stay in the **United States** with her family?

If you enjoy the nice life you have already experienced in America and want to stay permanently, turn to page 15.

If you agree to stay just temporarily, while working in some way to help the new country of Israel, turn to page 92.

15

You resign as an officer in the Israeli air force and remain in the **United States**. Your wife's father has a business in **Brownsville, Texas**, a dusty town on the **Rio Grande**, just across the border from **Mexico**. Every day, trucks arrive from farther north, loaded with goods that will be exported to **Mexico**. Other trucks pull into his parking lot with products that were made south of the border. The work is not difficult, and you and your wife are happy, especially as your family increases, first with a daughter, then with a son.

You are happy . . . except that you really miss Israel. Living in **Texas** has been good to you, but the Land of Israel is different. You can't explain how, but it just seems more like home. Each year, when you and your family go there for a visit, you find it harder and harder to leave.

One **Shabbat** morning, you are sitting in the little synagogue of **Brownsville**, listening to Mr. Perl, the member of the congregation who leads the services, when someone dashes into the sanctuary. "Stop the services!" he yells. "Israel has attacked the Arab countries. They had massed their troops on Israel's borders, but they never dreamed we would attack first. It looks like a great victory is about to occur." The prayers switch from those of the holiday to intense pleas for Israel's safety, and then, as if by a prearranged signal, everyone stands to sing "**Hatikvah**."

You turn to your wife. Without even saying a word, she nods. "I am afraid, but you must go at once. The air force will need you to help protect the country. Let's go home so you can pack and say good-bye to the children."

*If you enter the air war over the **Golan Heights** immediately, turn to page 99.*

If something delays your combat involvement, turn to page 100.

16

These people don't look like Jews. Tall, handsome, but very black, they seem more African than Jewish to you. Curious, you engage one of their men in conversation, and he tells you that they come from the Commandment Keepers Synagogue in **Harlem, New York**. "We have considered ourselves **Orthodox** Jews since about 1920," he tells you, "and we are just as excited about returning to the Land of Israel as Jews from other communities."

A heated debate erupts in the town. Are these men, women, and children really Jews? Did they convert *k'halachah*, according to strict Jewish law, or did one of their ancestors just decide one day to say he was a Jew? Contrary to your worst suspicions, it's not a debate about race, about whether black people can be Jews. Quite another issue is at stake: what makes a person a Jew? And if you are not born a Jew, how do you become Jewish?

This is not an insignificant issue. If these people are Jews, they are entitled to many rights under the **Law of Return**. They will be given housing, support, schooling, and jobs. If they are gentiles, they are still welcome, but under different conditions. The attacks are vehement, but so is the defense.

You anxiously await the decision of the rabbinate. If you think they will decide to call these immigrants Jews, turn to page 133.

If you are, on the other hand, dismayed that the debate is so nasty and that racial overtones have become part of it, turn to page 71.

17

It is clear to you that the best way to continue your search for answers is to become a **Reform** Jewish rabbi. **Nelson Glueck**'s archaeological school on **King David Street** now has added a program to train Israelis for this career. Unfortunately, you are also too old for the program, and the dean informs you as gently as possible that you will not be admitted.

Then he offers you something you had not expected. "I notice that you have a young man accompanying you. Do you suppose that he might be interested in our school?" You had not thought about the possibility that your grandson could become a rabbi, but when you discuss it with him over a **falafel** sandwich at an outdoor café on **Ben Yehuda Street**, you are amazed to discover that he has already considered the idea. Just finished with his own compulsory military service, he asks many of the same questions that the other war veterans posed, and he, too, thinks that the **Reform** Jewish movement will guide him toward the answers.

He enrolls in a joint program of the **Hebrew University** on **Mount Scopus** and the **Hebrew Union College–Jewish Institute of Religion**. When he completes his studies, the *rosh yeshivah* places his hands on your grandson's shoulders and ordains him a rabbi. After the services, you approach this handsome, intelligent young man with a huge smile and tears of joy running down your face. With your own hands on his shoulders, you pray for God's special blessings for his future. *Y'varech'cha Adonai v'yishm'recha* . . . may God always bless you and keep you . . . Amen.

END

18

When your daughter and son-in-law arrive in **Johannesburg**, their friends pick them up at the airport and drive them to a beautiful home with dark green lawns and a high fence around the yard. "We don't have homes like this in Israel. We live in a two-bedroom apartment on the side of a rocky hill." "Well, things are different here."

The next morning, their driver takes you out to see the diamond mines and the townships of **Soweto** where the African workers live. The contrast is immense. These poor people live in shacks made of flattened tin cans and whatever boards they can find. There is no electricity or running water or indoor plumbing.

That night as the group gathers for dinner, your son-in-law raises a delicate question. "Shouldn't we learn something from Jewish history? It looks to me that there is a coming revolution; the black people of this region will not accept these living conditions for much longer. Everything I know says that they will rise up against the white population and that the Jews of **South Africa** will get caught in between the two groups. Blacks will see Jews as white oppressors; whites will think of Jews as traitors who are generally supportive of the blacks. Either way, the future of the Jewish community of **South Africa** looks dangerous to me."

If you begin a project that might reduce hatred of Jews, turn to page 104.

*If you look for a way to protect the Jews of **South Africa**, turn to page 111.*

19

One thing you have learned from all your experiences: a person should not try to make major decisions when everything in life is uncertain. You were forced to make choices about how to survive during the war, then in the **displaced persons' camps**, then when you first came to Israel. Most of these decisions turned out well, but you never trusted them at the time. You certainly did not have the time to think clearly about them. Now that you are faced with a question that involves not just you but the security of the entire Jewish state, you really need a chance to consider all the options carefully.

That means finding a secure place to live. You cannot place your family at risk. It would be dangerous to make the wrong decision with them living in an exposed town, a place where the wrong move could backfire, could have serious consequences for them. You might make a bad choice if you were thinking of your family's personal safety, not of the welfare of the entire country.

You must find a place, then, that will never be given to the Arabs under any peace plan, where your family can live in peace and safety. To find such a place, turn to page 160.

20

Y ou assumed that sensible people could always sit around a table, drink a little coffee, and work out a solution to just about any problem or difference of opinion. But you had not understood the rigid strength of those people who think that they, and only they, have the right answer—and that any other solution is a sin. You find out about such individuals rather quickly.

On **Shabbat** afternoon, you are walking near the **Meah Shearim** section of the city when you hear a commotion. A large group of black-hatted, bearded **Chasidic** Jews surges forward toward the street. From the sidewalk, a hail of stones arches forward toward the passing cars. A few windows are broken, and there is a small accident as one driver loses control and runs into another car. "Aha!" crows one of the stone throwers. "That's the reward you get when you violate **Shabbes**. The Torah says 'Don't drive on **Shabbes**.' He did not obey *HaShem*. He deserves what he got!"

You try to reason with these men. After all, the road on which the cars were driving is on public property, outside their neighborhood. But they will not listen to your point of view. "To drive on **Shabbes** is a *chilul HaShem*, an insult to God. There can be no discussion about this. It is the truth. Our *rebbe* taught us that, and our *rebbe* is always right. That's all there is to it!"

*If your hopes for a peaceful **Jerusalem** are frustrated but you want to find a way to understand what these people believe, turn to page 136.*

If you cannot see their viewpoint at all, turn to page 137.

21

You and a team of Israeli agricultural specialists travel to **N'Djamena**, capital of the African nation of **Chad**. Other groups go to **Mali** and to **Niger**. Just to reach these countries is a long and difficult journey. There are some countries in **Africa** that will not permit Israeli aircraft to fly through their airspace, and others where the threat of terrorist attack is so great that you cannot land there to refuel. But after what seems an endless trek, your plane touches down.

This dry and dusty land lies on the southern fringe of the **Sahara Desert**. Even Israel's **Negev** has more vegetation than this place, and immediately you understand why there is a problem of hunger and starvation among the native population. There simply is no way, using traditional methods of farming, that they can produce enough food to feed their people.

A caravan of jeeps drives you away from the city, out into the countryside. There, you come to a small town where a group of village leaders have gathered to meet with you. You tell them about the drip irrigation method and show them the tubes and pictures of your test plot before and after you used this system. You tell them that Israel is prepared to give them the tubing and help them use the equipment, but that they will need to do the actual work. "That way, you will learn how. When we go back to our country, you will be able to continue." They nod their heads in agreement.

*If you have a surprising Jewish experience while you are in **Chad**, turn to page 78.*

If, when you return to Israel, you bring back unusual souvenirs, turn to page 79.

22

You are no longer as strong and vigorous as the young soldiers who walk alongside you, but your military commander thinks your maturity and good sense will be very important to them. The region of **Hebron** that you are patrolling has always been a hot spot for conflict, and the generals know that trouble could erupt at any moment. If it does, they want someone with a cool head and good judgment to make decisions.

Tensions have been increasing in recent weeks, as an Israeli firebrand, **Rabbi Meir Kahane**, and the local leaders of the **Palestine Liberation Organization (PLO)** have exchanged heated words. **Kahane** says that there can be no peace as long as Palestinian Arabs live in **Greater Israel**. A new political movement, **Gush Emunim**, has sprung up around him, composed mostly of the residents of new settlements that the Israeli government has established on the **West Bank**. The Arabs hate these settlements. "This is our land," they say. "There can be no peace until these Israeli intruders are removed."

Between **Kahane** and the **PLO** there is no room for compromise. Neither one of them will budge at all; all they will swap is angry words. Threats of violence are spoken daily, and that is why your patrol now walks this dusty road, only twenty or so miles south of **Jerusalem**. As you round the bend, you hear what you feared most—rifle shots. Your men grasp their weapons nervously and turn in the direction of the gunfire. "All right," you say. "Careful! Let's do what we were trained to do. Forward march!"

*If you want to try and understand those who support **Kahane**, turn to page 175.*

If you want to discover the source of the gunfire, turn to page 176.

23

Even in its earliest years, you can sense that Israel will be a country that depends on technology. Science and engineering will be vital, especially in the defense industries and in turning the desert into fertile farmland. You spend evenings with these bright young immigrants, persuading them to be part of Israel's technological future. They must raise their sights; making jewelry may have been enough of a challenge for their fathers, but it surely is only a start for them.

A new university has been opened in **Ramat Gan**, a suburb of **Tel Aviv**. The Mizrachi movement, made up of **Orthodox Zionists**, has created this school so that young men and women from very traditional backgrounds can study the most modern subjects at the same time that they continue to observe Judaism in a traditional way. This is exactly the place where these **Sephardic** young people can study without abandoning their religious practices or beliefs. What a wonderful opportunity for them!

Two of the young people with whom you are working become enthusiastic about the opportunity of studying at Bar Ilan University. One afternoon, you pile them into your car and drive down the coast to visit the campus. While you are there, you just happen to visit the admissions department, and you just happen to meet a counselor who is a friend of yours, and she just happens to greet these young people with warmth and excitement. "We can't wait until you become students at our school. You'll fit right in. "

One of your students decides that a technical career is not the right choice. To find out what occupation he chooses, turn to page 45.

But the other student agrees with you. She enrolls in one of the scientific programs at the university. To see where this path leads her, turn to page 46.

24

Immigrants are flooding into Israel. Not just survivors of the European wars, but hundreds of thousands who have been displaced from Arab lands. They come from different backgrounds. They speak **Yiddish**, Russian, Arabic, and **Ladino**. Some are highly educated people; some can barely read. Some are modern and sophisticated in every sense, and some do not know what electricity and running water are.

What they all have in common is that they have come to a new land, a Jewish land, in search of a better life for themselves and their children. They have sacrificed a chance to grow old in places that were familiar in favor of the opportunity to make a new and Jewish society. But before all of this wonderful promise can begin to be realized, they must have the necessities of life: food and housing. Food there is, provided by many international and Israeli relief agencies. Housing? Ha! That's another story. Where will these armies of immigrants find secure and healthy homes? Right now, they are living in tents provided by Tzahal, the Israeli army, but these are only a temporary solution.

A problem of this size can only be solved by the government—or an organization as big as the government. You turn to the director of **Solel Boneh**, the construction arm of the Histadrut. This is the biggest building company in Israel. If any group can erect housing for these immigrants, it is **Solel Boneh**. The director agrees with your idea, but he has an even better proposal. "To build small apartment buildings will never get the job done. What we need to do is create brand-new cities. We shall call them 'development towns,' and it will be there that the immigrants will settle."

If you agree to move to one of these new towns, turn to page 74.

If you think about moving to one of these new towns, but get sidetracked, turn to page 42.

25

You understand that **Reform** Jews study history seriously; that's how they discover how their religion has changed and grown over the centuries, and that's how they make decisions about what to do in today's world. But you are not sure that you need an organized religion to teach you about history. Every walk you take in **Jerusalem** follows the path of historical characters; every step you take places your feet in the footsteps of **Abraham and Sarah, Jeremiah**, and **Yochanan ben Zakkai**. The kings and the priests and the prophets of ancient Judah walked where you do now.

The man who governs this city, **Teddy Kollek**, is as remarkable as the city itself. Every day, he strides through its streets, talking to the residents, working to make the city more beautiful and special. He has a vision that he shares with you one evening. "I want **Jerusalem** to become the real city of peace. That is, after all, what its name means. I want my city to demonstrate how the finest Jewish values can be brought down from the heavenly **Jerusalem** and made real in the earthly city. Did not the **prophet Isaiah** [2:3] teach us that the word of the Lord must go forth from **Jerusalem**? I mean to make that prophecy come true."

Kollek's vision is infectious. You are captured by it and become a member of the team that manages the city's affairs. But you discover, almost immediately, that it is easier to dream this dream than to make it pass into reality.

If you spend a lot of your time dealing with conflicts among the different Jewish communities that make up the city's population, turn to page 20.

If an outside threat becomes your preoccupation, turn to page 127.

26

To find out more about **kibbutz** life, you travel to the southern tip of the **Sea of Galilee**. **Degania**, the first collective settlement dating all the way back to 1910, is a place where you can learn what this kind of life is all about.

An older man sits down with you in the dining hall. "Forty years ago, I lived in a little town in the **Ukraine**. There was an active **Zionist** youth group in our village, and every so often one of its members would leave and go to Palestine. I was one of those young people. I came here a long time ago and settled here at **Degania**. Let me tell you. Life was rough. There were mosquitoes that gave us malaria and Arabs who attacked us and never enough food and backbreaking work. But we were all comrades together, and we did what we had to do and we made a success. That's what collective living is all about—working with your friends to achieve a common goal. Oh, we made lots of sacrifices, but it was all worthwhile in the end because we kept our beliefs and ideals intact."

You wonder if there are still settlements where this pioneer spirit continues. If you set out to find one, turn to page 186.

*If, on the other hand, you think a more modern **kibbutz** might suit you better, turn to page 32.*

27

In a beautiful, large park not far from the center of **Moscow**, a park dedicated to the memory of the victims of World War II, you find a monument. Surrounding the monument are three houses of prayer: a church, a mosque, and a synagogue. As interesting as the other two are, you cannot resist entering the synagogue, and there you find a small group of people praying. You have heard about this synagogue. Others have told you that the Judaism practiced there has the potential to help many Russian Jews come back to Judaism.

Standing next to an older couple, you overhear the husband speaking to his wife. "Look at the *siddur*. Do you see how it is different from the one I learned from when I was a little boy? That one said that we should thank God that we have not been created as women. But here it says *she-asani Yisrael;* 'Thank You, God, for making me Jewish.' That's so much more positive. Besides, how could I sit next to you and pray if I were to say what we used to say? That would not be very respectful of you." And his wife leans closer, puts her arm through his, and sings the prayers in unison with her husband.

In your youth in **Poland** you never experienced this kind of Judaism. In Israel you were so busy that you never found such a Jewish faith. How strange it is, then, that you have had to come back to **Eastern Europe** to learn about liberal Judaism! You weep silently, tears of happiness. It has taken a long time, and the road has been long and twisted. But, finally, you have found a way to be Jewish that makes you feel at home. *"Baruch atah Adonai,"* you chant, *"she-asani Yisrael.* Thank You, God, that You have made it possible for me to be this kind of Jew. Amen."

END

28

Everywhere there is suspicion. Anyone can be denounced and arrested. As a foreigner and as a Jew, you are especially suspect. You sense wary eyes turning to follow you, even when you walk down the street or go to the market to buy some food.

You were not wrong to be afraid. One day, as you stride across the great square in front of the **Kremlin** towers, three very large men approach you. "You will come with us," they say. You have no choice; there is no way to resist their order. You find yourself shoved roughly into a cell in the dreaded **Lubyanka** prison. All you did was watch the traditional May Day parade, but men have died here for less. Horrible tales of torture and killing are told of this fortress, and you are literally terrified about your future. For several days, you are left alone, your only company the hand of a jailer who shoves a bowl of gruel and a piece of black bread under your door once a day.

Then—you have no idea whether it is day or night or even how many days have passed—a key turns in the lock and the door is opened. Two guards grab you by the arms and hurry you up some stairs and into a large room. There, to your great relief, you see your superior from the Israeli embassy.

The Russian commissar speaks sternly. "There is no place for someone like you in our country. But, luckily, you are protected as a diplomat. You have exactly twenty-four hours to be out of **Russia**!" Your boss nods briefly and gestures to you to keep quiet. You really didn't need that warning! You entered Palestine in 1947, and you felt happy; but Israel will never seem as good as it will when you get home this time.

*If you plan to find an interesting job in a suburb of **Tel Aviv**, turn to page 139.*

If you decide that you want to learn more about ancient Israel, turn to page 140.

29

When she graduates from high school, your daughter enlists in the air force. For her, this is more than her required military service; to be a career pilot and officer is all she has ever wanted. But the air force assigns her to the communication section. They are not sure that a woman ought to be a pilot, especially in a combat aircraft. Old attitudes die a slow death, and the officers in charge of selecting recruits for pilot training have not yet freed themselves from long-held prejudices.

She is angry, really angry. You can see her rage as she slices through the **challah** at your **Shabbat** meal one Friday night. If the bread had been the general in charge of assignments, she would have cut him in half!

"I won't accept their judgment. What they are offering is not good enough. I want to be a pilot, and I will be a pilot. If I cannot fulfill this ambition in the air force, I'll find another way. But this group of old men will not stop me! Never!"

To see if she can achieve her goal, turn to page 56.

30

Y ou consult with the leaders of the **Rabbanut**. That's important, because in a matter like this, their decision is likely to carry
a lot of weight. "On the one hand," they tell you, "Brother Daniel
converted to Catholicism. So long as there was danger, he had
the right to do whatever was necessary to save his own life. But,
after the war was over and he could have returned safely to
Judaism, he chose not to. Because he stayed Catholic, it is
possible that he is no longer a Jew and not entitled to the
citizenship offered under the **Law of Return**. Still," they continue, "he did try to save some of the Jews of **Poland**." (You can
appreciate that, given your own experiences.) "And he was born
of a Jewish mother. Therefore, is he not still a Jew?"

Emotionally, you have to side with Brother Daniel. Anyone who would risk his life to save fellow Jews as he did ought
to be entitled to a lot of consideration. But legally—and you are
being asked to be his attorney—you don't know whether he has
much of a leg to stand on. You also wonder whether you might,
as a fellow survivor of the war in Europe, be a little too
personally involved to handle the case.

You decide not to become Brother Daniel's lawyer, but you
follow the case carefully in the newspapers.

*If you try to help him in his quest for citizenship in
some other way, turn to page 64.*

*If you prefer to seek honor for this man in a very
special manner, turn to page 110.*

31

As the plane circles overhead, you think, "One day, perhaps our daughter could be a pilot. Someone has to fly those craft. On the other hand, someone must also design and build them. Right now, we are buying all our planes from Boeing in America. But we cannot allow ourselves to be so totally dependent on foreigners, as friendly as they might be. There could come a time when they might not be as well-disposed to us as they are now. No! We must develop our own aircraft industry."

Your daughter agrees with you. "*Abba*, that is a great idea. I'm going to do it." She enrolls as an engineering student at the University of Washington in **Seattle**. Being close to Boeing's headquarters will give her the best training possible. Even during the summer vacation, she cannot rest. She arranges a job in the Boeing aircraft plant at **Everett, Washington**, so that she can see how airplanes are built from inside out.

When she graduates, she returns to help create Israel's own aircraft industry. What a vital role she will play in ensuring the security and independence of this country! When she comes home from work, she turns to you with gratitude. "You gave me a great idea. I am so thankful that you have directed me along this path. It's as though you yourself wrote **King Solomon**'s proverb 'Train up a child in the way she should go, and even when she is older, she will not depart from it' [Proverbs 22:6]. You led me to the right path. I promise you, I shall never depart from it."

Nothing could make your heart more glad than to hear words like these from your own daughter. She will carry on your values; you will live on through her deeds. And this awareness gives you peace beyond description. You are thoroughly content.

END

32

OK, so you don't want to live in a tent and work like a slave from dawn until dusk. Is there anything wrong with wanting to live with a few comforts, especially given all you've gone through in your life and that you are now no longer a youngster? You don't think so, and you set out to find a **kibbutz** that still believes in **socialism**, but has become established enough to provide its members with a higher standard of living.

The site on which you settle is called **Ein Gedi**. It is located on the western shore of the **Dead Sea**. Nearly two thousand years ago, **Simeon bar Kochba**, the Jewish leader who led an armed rebellion against the Romans, made this place his headquarters. And you can understand why. Even though it is very hot during the summer, there are beautiful palm trees, and people say that the salty water of the **Dead Sea** can heal many ailments. Just the smell of all those chemical salts ought to cure something!

Like all **kibbutzim**, the property of **Ein Gedi** belongs to all members equally. But here there is a lot of property. The **kibbutz** has decided to create a health resort for Israelis, and they have built hotels, restaurants, and a beach house. A casino for gambling is even planned. This is hardly the **kibbutz** that the grandfather at **Degania** told you about. Why, this **kibbutz** even hires some of the local Arab men and women to help with their work.

You settle in **Ein Gedi** and marry. Soon, you are raising a fine family. As your son grows toward adulthood, you wonder if he will stay here to continue the work you have begun.

To find out what he decides, turn to page 33.

33

Your son dislikes **kibbutz** life. Even the constant excitement of tourists arriving at **Ein Gedi** cannot compare for him to walking down **Dizengoff Street** in **Tel Aviv** or sitting at an open-air café on **Ben Yehudah Street** in **Jerusalem**. He craves the action of the city. There seems to be little that you can do to stop him from settling in one of Israel's larger centers. Nothing is likely to change his mind.

But something does. Arab terrorists explode a car bomb near the main bus station in **Tel Aviv**. It seems that these militant Palestinian Arabs have lost faith in negotiations for Palestinian independence and think that they can force Israel to recognize a Palestinian state by acts of terror. But Israelis won't be bullied into this kind of decision. They will only vote for a Palestinian state if they are convinced it is the right move.

But your son, living now just a few blocks from the bomb blast, is frightened. *"Abba,"* he asks, "has anything like that happened in **Ein Gedi**?" "No," you reply. "Not in the last several thousand years since the time of **Bar Kochba**!"

A little reluctantly, he moves home. Clearly, he would have preferred to stay in the city, but the safer life of the desert **kibbutz** is now appealing. It's a trade-off, a compromise in which he gives up one good thing to achieve a different positive goal. And, at least, he can still walk the streets talking on his portable telephone and surf the computer Internet at home in the evening.

You and your wife are very happy. Your children may not really understand why it is special to live on a **kibbutz**, but at least they are at home and safe. For you as parents, there is little that is more important than that.

END

34

As you reflect on the issue, you wonder if the **Orthodox** rabbinate is not right in the long run. Perhaps there should be only one definition of what it means to be a Jew, one way to become a Jew if you are not born one. To have two kinds of conversions would mean to have two different kinds of Jews. You are not sure that this is a very good idea at all.

You sit with your future son-in-law in the living room of your apartment and talk seriously. "Would it be so terrible if you went to the **Rabbanut** and went through a second conversion, this one under **Orthodox** supervision? I know that you won't ever be an **Orthodox** Jew; neither am I. But to preserve a single Jewish people, what would it hurt?"

He agrees and makes an appointment. You wait anxiously for him to report back, but you can tell as he rounds the corner with a vigorous stride that things did not go well. Actually, he is furious. "Can you believe that they told me I would have to study for two years, observe **Shabbat** in the **Orthodox** manner, keep kosher—all of that, and then maybe, only maybe, they would consider approving my conversion. What an insult!"

You feel the pain this young man has gone through. He has tried so hard to fit in, and he has been kicked in the teeth. You hate to see someone hurt like this, and he is almost a member of your family. You may be right in theory that one people, one conversion is the right thing. But there has to be a better way in practice.

*If you decide to learn more about **Orthodox** Judaism and its rigid approach, turn to page 184.*

If you choose to find another approach for your future son-in-law, turn to page 84.

35

The more you explore the life of a **kibbutznik**, the less it seems to fit your personal needs. You have spent your entire life in poverty, first in the *shtetl* in **Poland** where you were born, then in the camps, finally trying to get established in Israel. Now that you are finally free and able to earn a decent living, you don't want the proceeds of your labor to go to someone else. Your money belongs to you; you have a right to enjoy it.

There may be another, better option for you; something between a collective **kibbutz** and a capitalist, individual life in the city. This choice is the **moshav**, a settlement where everyone keeps his or her own property, but where decisions are made together. You are particularly drawn to this kind of experimental community because Israel is now building groups of them to accommodate new immigrants from **North Africa**. Just to the north of the desert city of **Beersheva**, a group of five **moshav** settlements is rising from the sand. Immigrants from **Tunisia** will inhabit one; those from **Morocco** will be in another; **sabra**s, native-born Israelis, will live in a third. You choose the **moshav** called **Zohar**, where most of the people are refugees from **Romania**. You imagine that you will have more in common with them than with the **Sephardic** neighbors, although you love to go over to the other settlements and listen to their music and eat their spicy food.

Unfortunately, your idea that you would fit in with the Romanians doesn't work out. Their style of life and yours are not the same, and it soon becomes apparent that you will have to find another place to live. You've had enough of the desert heat, so your new location needs to be up in the north. But where?

*You might look for a location on the **Golan**. To move there, turn to page 82.*

*Another possibility is the region of **Dan**. To go there, turn to page 88.*

36

Y ou stand with your daughter under the *chuppah* and weep tears of joy. Only a few decades ago, you despaired of even living. Now, your daughter is married, and a bright future lies ahead for her and her new husband. Their life will not be yours, thank God. You suffered much, but you have triumphed. Now, it is her turn to make her mark on the world.

One of the ways she makes a mark is through a son of her own and then a second child, a beautiful daughter. These children grow up entirely in Israeli society. They speak Hebrew, but they are learning English, like almost all the children here. They can kick a soccer ball and hike in the desert, but just as easily sit down and program a computer. It's a new generation.

Your grandson is restless. He wants a different kind of life in Israel, one that is more active and more exciting. To follow him to a new place, turn to page 33.

Your granddaughter is different. She is fascinated by the record of the Jewish past. When her school class takes a trip to **Poland**, she is less interested in **Auschwitz** (even though that's where you were a prisoner) than in listening to the folk music of the region. As she descends from the airplane at Ben-Gurion Airport, she is humming a melody that you recognize from your childhood.

"Grandpa, this is what I think I have to do. I shall go to the university and study music, especially the music of the Jewish past. If we are to keep our heritage alive, the sounds of our people must be preserved."

If she continues in the field of ethnomusicology,
turn to page 134.

If she finds another musical outlet, turn to page 187.

Y ou look over the small plot of land that you have washed and feel a strong sense of satisfaction. After thousands of years, the evil of **Sodom** has finally been purged. The curse that God cast upon this region may now have been removed, and perhaps the time has come for the land to come back to life.

You would love to plant fruit trees in this ground. But it is really too hot for apples or pears, and you really need plants that will stop the erosion of the soil from wind and the occasional rainstorm that hits this area. Besides, it takes three or four years for saplings to mature and produce fruit. You need crops that will prove your experiment worthwhile in a much shorter time. An agricultural scientist suggests that you think about what the Israelites might have eaten as they were fleeing from **Egypt**. Great idea! The Bible does tell you that they liked onions, cucumbers, leeks, beans, and other vegetables. If those plants could have grown in the **Sinai** during the Exodus, perhaps they could still grow in the area under the right conditions.

With your helpers, you plant row upon row of seeds, some of them carefully placed in little mounds of dirt. Sprinklers keep the ground moist. Impatiently, you come out three or four times each day, looking for any sign of growth. Finally, after about two weeks, you bend down and then let out a yell. "There are little green sprouts growing in our garden. We have succeeded. The desert is coming back to life." But, of course, you also realize that it has taken a tremendous amount of water to produce this result. Another group of farm researchers near **Jericho** has come up with a way to save water.

To learn from them, turn to page 6.

38

For several months, you crisscross the **United States**, speaking at Jewish community centers and synagogues. Everywhere you go, large crowds of Jews gather to support the protest against the proposed **Knesset** action. When they hear what you say, they are moved to write letters, and some even join community missions to Israel where they can meet with Israeli leaders and express their points of view.

As you return home on **El Al**, you think about these remarkable assemblies. You realize that you have the power to persuade other people to act. It is this realization that draws you into the political world. You run for a seat in the **Knesset** and are elected as a member of a small party, Meretz. On the face of it, this party is too small to make a difference. But, because the larger parties are not big enough to form a majority government on their own, they must make coalition agreements with some of the smaller parties, and this gives Meretz and other parties like it much greater power. Without you and your two colleagues, there will be no stable government. To convince you to join the government, however, the Labor Party must agree to drop the proposed change in the **Law of Return**.

You realize, of course, that the issue is only dead temporarily. It will come back. But you will serve as a member of the **Knesset** as long as you can, and you will help others who agree with you. With this bloc of votes, you will be able to make a real difference in the future of Israel, and that makes you very satisfied.

END

39

This, you conclude, is not an issue that will be decided by one **Knesset** vote or another. What is really at stake is the long-range nature of Israel as a society. As you sip a cup of coffee with your friends one evening, they ask the important questions: "Who are we as a people? Are we all the same, all **Orthodox**? Or are there many different kinds of Jews in Israel? And if there are, shouldn't those who are not **Orthodox** gain some strength?"

You understand how right this idea is. If the views of the 70 percent of Israeli citizens who are not **Orthodox** are to be heard, then the religious movements that would be most attractive to these people must become larger and stronger. You cannot just depend on pressure from the **Diaspora**. Israel must be governed by its own citizens; Israelis themselves must decide what it will mean to be a Jew in the Jewish state.

At headquarters of the **Israel Movement for Progressive Judaism**, you offer your help. "We shall need to build congregations and schools, especially schools for very young children; we need members and even our own leaders. One day, we shall even have **Reform** rabbis educated and ordained in Israel."

You respond to these ideas with enthusiasm. Others can be involved in politics. Building Israel's liberal Jewish movement becomes your passion. Within only a few years, you sit on the patio wall at **Hebrew Union College–Jewish Institute of Religion** on **King David Street** and watch as the first Israeli young man becomes a **Reform** rabbi. What a glorious day this is! Your work is not complete, but you have made immense progress, and you are very confident that this is absolutely the right direction.

END

40

It's a little embarrassing. You are too old to go on a difficult and taxing mission to **Africa**; that task will be undertaken by younger men and women. But you realize that you have done your part. You have helped develop new techniques in agriculture that will feed many, and you have helped build up your own new land, the State of Israel.

Thanks to people like you—and you are not so modest as to deny this accomplishment—Israel can now grow its own food, export many items to other countries, and perhaps most important, teach people in other countries how to use modern, scientific farming methods to feed themselves.

But food is only the most basic ingredient for a new nation. It is certainly not enough. You remember what the biblical **prophet Zechariah** [4:6] once said: "Not by might nor by power, but by My spirit, said the Lord of Hosts." As far back as the time of the Bible, even God recognized that more is needed to build a country than food and houses, roads and buildings, factories and armies. A long time ago, this **prophet** told his Jewish audience that the most essential thing a people must have is a common way of thinking about life, a culture that they all share, a view of the world based on spiritual and religious ideas.

If you believe that Israel needs an institution that will help develop this kind of common bond of culture, turn to page 128.

If there is something you always wanted to do, but never had the time, and you believe that doing this will create a common Israeli culture, turn to page 130.

41

"If we can't get married in Israel the way we want," your future daughter-in-law sobs, "let's go back to the synagogue in America where I grew up. At least my family is there, and my rabbi will do the ceremony. He officiated at my bat mitzvah and confirmation, and he got me to go to the camp where I first was bitten by the **kibbutz** ideal. It just seems right." What a good idea! You and your family have never visited **North America**; now you have a great reason to make the trip.

The wedding is gorgeous, and you feel almost at once that you are a member of this community. Everyone is friendly, and it is hard to leave and move on to the vacation travels that you had planned. "We'll see you back in **Yahel**," you yell out the car window, as you drive away from her family's home. "We love you. *Mazal tov!*"

But back in Israel nothing seems quite right, especially to the new young couple. They feel that their Jewish choices have been rejected by their country. This leaves them with a bad feeling. "If Israel cannot respect our Jewish style, then perhaps we do not belong here," they wonder. Soon, their doubts become more solid. After a year of wrestling with the questions, they decide that they cannot remain in Israel, and they leave, moving away from Israel to the lands of the **Diaspora**.

Yet they will always be Israelis in some sense. Their commitment to the building of the Jewish homeland continues, as they devote a great deal of their time to speaking in schools and churches and civic clubs about Israel. They tell you, "We may not be able to live in Israel until the religious situation is changed, but we shall always support Israel. Even if we do not always like what Israel does, it will always be our homeland, too."

END

42

Y̱ou board the Egged bus at the main transit station in **Jerusalem** and settle into your seat for the long drive down the **Judean Hills**. Your seat mate is a young woman who tells you that she made *aliyah* about three years ago. Her "typical" American-Jewish family lived in a suburb of a large city—two cars, nice house, trips to the mall, vacations—a normal life. But something was missing. At the summer camp of her synagogue's youth movement, she loved learning Hebrew and living in the tents of the camp **kibbutz**. "It was so much fun sharing everything, working together, not having to compete with my friends about who was more popular or who had better clothes or stuff like that. It seemed so real, not false like the high school I went to at home."

As the two of you talk, the miles pass quickly. Somewhere around **Ein Gedi**, your new friend turns to you and says: "I have a great idea. Why don't you come to visit our **kibbutz**? It is the first **Reform** Jewish settlement of its kind in the world. We call it **Yahel**, and we are trying to mix the best of collective life with the best of liberal Jewish religion. We also work very hard in the fields, but you'll be amazed at the beauty of the flowers that we raise."

It's an idea that you cannot dismiss. And so you decide to stay at **Yahel**, not just for a short visit but permanently, if your family will agree. In fact, it is such a wonderful place that when your wife and your son, now in his twenties, come down to visit, they agree to make the move. Soon, the crystal-clear desert air, the enthusiasm and idealism of the **kibbutzniks**, and the hard but rewarding work bring you a sense of renewed life. It was a great choice.

*If **Yahel** also proves a great choice for your son, turn to page 158.*

If the manager of the greenhouse brings you a problem, turn to page 5.

43

Archaeology sounds OK, but do you really want to spend your life digging up the remains of people who died three thousand years ago? Aren't the concerns of today's Jews more important? As you ask yourself these questions, the answer comes clear: what happens in the modern world interests you far more than what occurred long ago.

And this is especially true because of the **Yom Kippur War**. On October 6, 1973, while the Jews of Israel were praying in their synagogues, the armies of **Egypt** and **Syria** mounted a surprise attack across the **Suez Canal** and into the **Golan Heights**. Ultimately, fighter jets from the Israeli air force and tanks from the army turn the initial setbacks into victories, but thousands of young Israelis die defending their country.

As the soldiers return from the war, they begin to ask difficult questions. They wonder whether war is really the answer to the political differences of the Middle East, whether more of their friends will have to die in another conflict, whether there is any meaning to the death of the young people who fought with them. Life, they have discovered, can be taken from them in an instant; what makes life really worthwhile and valuable? What would they give up their lives for? Is there anything so important that they would willingly pay the ultimate price for it?

You sit for hours with these combat veterans, talking about these very deep concerns. You cannot stop thinking about their questions. You must find a way to use whatever years are left in your own life to help them make sense of the questions that came out of their war experience. You are passionately committed to this quest.

If you think you might find answers in the clear desert air, turn to page 59.

But if you believe you need to take a different route in search of answers, turn to page 17.

44

One of the most active programs in all of **Russia** is the **Chabad**. The initials making up this name stand for Hebrew words meaning "wisdom," "understanding," and "knowledge." **Chabad** is a program directed by the **Lubavitch Chasidim**. These **Chasidic** Jews have made it their goal to reach out to Jews who are not **Orthodox** and teach them how to observe the **mitzvot** in the most traditional way possible.

Of course, they have opened synagogues and hold services every day. But they do so much more. Under **Chabad**'s management are programs to feed hungry people, teach children, and provide counseling for the confused and help for the sick. They have created a network of social services that extends the hand of kindness and assistance to any Jew, **Orthodox** or not, who needs their care. To be sure, they also want each Jew of **Russia** to observe Judaism in their way, the traditional way. But, while they wait and persuade, they do much good.

This is not your way of practicing Judaism. As an Israeli, even an Israeli who has been in **Russia** for a long time, you are not comfortable with a kind of Judaism that you consider "old-fashioned." But what you want for yourself is irrelevant. Better that the Jews of **Russia** become some kind of Jew than that they disappear from the Jewish map altogether. **Chabad** is offering something useful and important in the lives of many Russian Jews, and you are grateful that they are willing to help.

END

45

"**A** lot of people, like you, helped me get to Israel and then become a citizen. I am not sure that I could have settled here without all the assistance I received," this young, thoughtful man reflects about his experience. "It was difficult, coming to this new place, but so many people made it easy for me. Now I think I need to pay back some of the kindnesses that were extended to me. No! I can't really do anything for the people who helped me. But I can learn how to help the youngsters who will come in the next few years. Certainly, there will be lots of other immigrants. I shall study counseling and social work so that I can make their move to Israel even smoother than mine."

After he graduates from Bar Ilan University, he moves to a new development town in the far north of Israel, **Metulla**, a town where many new Israelis have decided to live. Some of their children, especially the teenagers, are having adjustment problems. They had to leave their homes and their friends, everything they were used to, when their families moved to Israel. Now, everything is brand new, and they are not sure how to manage in this new place.

This *madrich* goes into the high schools and sits down at the tables where some of these troubled teens eat lunch. He begins conversations with them. "I think I understand a little of what you are going through. After all, it was only a few years ago that I came to Israel." Slowly, he and the young people become friends. They accept his invitation to join the *tzofim*, the Israeli scouts, a youth movement that everyone admires.

*If he continues to live in **Metulla** and begins his family, turn to page 126.*

*If he watches as his **tzofim** grow up and enter the army, turn to page 177.*

46

Her family is not sure. Women in traditional Arab lands do not go to college and do not pursue careers. Jews who lived among these Arabs accepted the same values; their daughters were expected to be mothers and stay home. But this young woman shows remarkable promise. She is very bright and capable; her grades in school rank her at the top of her class. You persuade her parents that she is entitled to a chance, that in Israel women can have the same opportunities as men. Finally, they agree.

She enrolls at Bar Ilan University. It's comforting for her and her family that the university is sponsored by an **Orthodox** group. For her family to change its views about women's rights and then to send their daughter to a secular school would have been too much. This is a kind of compromise.

Within a year, she becomes fascinated with electricity. "Power is what makes things happen in this world. Computers, jet planes, cars—anything you can think of that really counts— all of these use electricity. This is what I want to learn about. If I become an electrical engineer, I can really make a difference!"

She graduates with a degree in electrical engineering, but that's not enough for this ambitious young immigrant. She continues her studies until she earns the degree of doctor of science. When she receives her diploma, her family greets her with immense pride. "Do you understand what an achievement this is?" her mother says. "In my generation, women could hardly read. Now, here you are, a scholar! We are so proud!"

If she decides to apply her new knowledge to the production of electrical power, turn to page 141.

If the need for water captures her interest, turn to page 142.

47

"My mother and father saved Jewish lives," your daughter tells her friends. "Now it is my turn to repeat the reception process. The Jews from **Yemen** no longer need me; they are here, settled, a segment of Israel that is growing in importance and strength. But there are other Jews in the world who desperately need our help. I shall not turn my back on them."

It does not take long to discover which Jews most need help. In the **Gondar** region of **Ethiopia**, tens of thousands of Jews live in primitive conditions. Some believe that they and their ancestors have lived in this area of **Africa** for more than two thousand years. That the kind of Judaism they observe is more like that of biblical times suggests that they have been cut off from Jewish life for a very long time.

Their situation is getting worse and worse as the war between **Ethiopia** and **Eritrea** spills over into their territory. Like the Yemenites before them, they must be gotten out, flown to Israel and resettled. Your daughter, to your immense pleasure and pride, becomes a leader in Operation Moses, the rescue of the Ethiopian Jews.

All that you and your wife have taught her, by direct teaching and by the example of your lives, continues in your daughter's passion for this task. Her values are your values, and you rejoice that the tradition will continue. The idea that *kol Yisrael areivin zeh lazeh*, that all Jews are responsible for the welfare of all other Jews, will persist unbroken into the next generation tells you that your lives have been enormously worthwhile.

END

48

Together—father, mother, and daughter—you create a center to teach Hebrew to newcomers to Israel. Whether they are permanent *olim* or visitors who will only stay six months or a year, they must know how to communicate. Without the language, they can never be a true part of Israeli society.

Sometimes it is tedious and boring to teach the same vocabulary and verb tables again and again. But over the **Shabbat** dinner table, when you and your family sing the familiar blessings, you always come back to the basic idea: language is the key to being a member of the community. Israel is composed of people who have come from the four corners of the earth. These immigrants grew up speaking many different languages and enjoying many different cultures. By teaching them Hebrew, you are helping them share one aspect of Israel that will be common to all of them; you are contributing to the creation of a single, unified nation.

In February of 1998, you receive a letter from the president of Israel. "On the occasion of the fiftieth anniversary of the creation of the modern State of Israel," it says, "I shall bestow a certificate of honor on those citizens who have been most influential in the forging of this country. You and your family have made just such a contribution. I invite you to my residence in **Jerusalem** on May 14, 1998, to receive this honor."

The three of you have worked as a family to build the Jewish homeland. Together, you make the pilgrimage to **Jerusalem**, and with eyes full of pride and happiness, you shake the president's hand and accept this special honor. Your life's work has been recognized as vitally important. And it's not over yet—there's more work to be done!

END

49

Working with the faculty of the **Technion**, you create a small panel, only a meter long and half a meter high. Several of these panels, linked together, could easily warm enough water for a family and heat a small home.

Soon, panels like these seem to grow on the roofs of apartment buildings throughout Israel. You are enormously glad to see that your fellow citizens are being helped by this invention. But that was not your real motive or goal. You had meant to export the new device to countries where very poor people might benefit from it.

With your colleagues, you look around for just such an opportunity. Suddenly, you get a brainstorm: we can trade the solar collectors for something Israel needs. Far to the west of Israel, the kingdom of **Morocco** is a place where both many Jews and many poor **Moslem** tribesmen live. The Jews want to emigrate to Israel, and Israel certainly would like to see them move to the Jewish state. On the other hand, the tribesmen in the Atlas Mountains could surely take advantage of your invention.

You travel to **Rabat** and meet with the advisers to the king. They think your plan would be good for their country in many ways, and the king agrees. Soon, the hills are dotted with solar collectors; inexpensive, renewable energy will shortly be available to many people. And the doors of emigration are wide open. Tens of thousands of Jews make *aliyah*. It was a little idea, but the payoff has been immense, and you spend the rest of your life knowing that your idea has helped many people in many, many ways.

END

50

Y ou march along the sidewalk outside the Ministry of Justice in **Jerusalem**. The sign you carry says simply "No more treason." A reporter from the newspaper *Haaretz* asks you what you mean by this placard. "This man gave away top-secret military information. That kind of treason has to stop! Never again will we permit Israel to be at a disadvantage if she is attacked by hostile neighbors."

You think back over your personal history. You suffered through the ***Shoah***, illegally entered Palestine, and then fought in the **War of Independence**. You sent your son and the sons of your friends to war in 1967 and again in 1973. Some of them died, and some of them were wounded. All of them were affected by the combat they saw.

Now, here is a scientist, perhaps a man with a conscience who thinks he is doing the right thing. But you disagree. He is hurting Israel's self-defense, and you have not lived through all that you have experienced now to allow Israel to be placed in danger. That's what you are convinced he has done—make it harder for Israel to defend itself.

If it is the last thing you do in your life, you will do whatever it takes to protect this precious Jewish state. *"**Am Yisrael chai**,"* you chant as you wave your sign in the air, "the people of Israel shall live forever."

END

51

You take a big bite of a red tomato, and its juice runs down your chin. There were no tomatoes in biblical times; they are a fruit that was discovered in the **New World**, but they taste so good that you couldn't resist planting a few vines and hoping that the crop would mature just as it has—red and juicy and just about as sweet as any fruit you know.

As you think about the deep red juice running down your face, you remember that you had seen red liquid on a human face sometime earlier in your life. In the concentration camps of World War II, you watched as **SS** guards beat Jewish prisoners with whips and sticks, and red blood flowed down their broken heads. In the Israeli **War of Independence** you watched again as young men and women were shot by Arab soldiers; their heads, too, were often covered with blood. The memory of this flowing red liquid brings salty tears to your eyes. Some of these people were your friends; some of them were even your family.

Now, however, you can smile. This red is different. The blood that flowed sapped the life from people, but this red gives life. This red juice is full of vitamins and minerals; someone with this red juice on the face will become healthy and strong.

And this life is not just for Jewish people. This is a gift for everyone, a gift you must find a way to share.

To do that, turn to page 21.

52

A team headed by the famous archaeologist **Avraham Biran** comes to **Dan** to examine this stone. Looking at it under a magnifying glass, they talk furiously among themselves. From the commotion, you know that this little stone must be something quite important. Finally, they turn to you. "We are very, very excited. What your son found has writing on it from the time of **King Solomon**. That means that it is almost three thousand years old. It was probably buried for all that time. Now, it has come to the surface. We suspect that there must be many more things from that period of biblical history right here. This could be a major discovery!"

Soon there is a full-scale archaeological dig at **Tel Dan**, the hump-shaped little hill near the spring and the trees. **Biran** guides his workers as they cut a trench. They explain that this pie-slice cut helps them see the inside of this hill from its top to its bottom. As the insides of the mound come into view, the workers dig very carefully. "Oh, my gosh! Oh, my gosh!" one of them exclaims, as she sweeps the loose dirt away from a piece of stone. This large, concave object has points at its four corners. "An ancient altar for sacrifices," **Biran** explains. "From the time of **King Solomon**. We have found the first biblical sanctuary that we can date to this very ancient time. What your son accidentally found has turned out to be a major historical site. We are very grateful to him—and to you."

As you and your family grow older, you often walk to the site of the dig. There, you can sense the connection of this place from today back over time for three thousand years. You feel completely at home, like you must belong to this place. You can never imagine living anywhere else.

END

53

What a surprise! Your daughter has grown into a lovely young woman, a woman with a mind of her own. She enters your workroom, holding hands with a young man you know very well. He is one of the students from **Yemen** you have helped teach in your classes. They have decided to marry, and they seek your blessing.

You think to yourself that in prewar Europe, this kind of mixing would not have been accepted. Why, they would not even allow a **Litvak** to marry a **Galitzianer**! But Israel is a new and different country. Maybe the old ways were not so good; maybe there are other values that are more important, such as whether they love each other and whether they can help build this country. You and your wife place your hands on their shoulders and tell them that you approve.

The young couple opens a shop where their fellow art students can exhibit their works for free and, occasionally, sell a piece. It is good that they have something positive to do with their art. But more important is the news that they bring you after the candles are lit one **Shabbat** evening. "We are going to have a baby!" You could not be more excited. And when your grandson is born, your life feels altogether complete. You came from the destruction of **Nazi** Europe. Now, you and your family are building a future in the Jewish state. "Praised are You, O God, who has blessed us with so many good things. Amen."

END

54

W hat an immense vision! **Glueck** thinks of a time when every future leader of the Jewish people will spend a year studying at the **Hebrew Union College–Jewish Institute of Religion** in this sacred city. "Wouldn't it change their hearts," he says, "if every day they could walk among the reminders of the Jewish past, in this city where the Jewish future is an ever-present fact. They would speak Hebrew more fluently, and they would be more attached in every way to our people."

Students come. First, the rabbinic students; then, cantorial and education and social work students. Teenagers on summer tours pass through the campus, and American college students from the **Hebrew University** spend time at the school. It becomes even more of a center than **Glueck** had ever imagined.

When you retire from your work with the school, the College-Institute holds a **Shabbat** morning service in your honor. As you sit in the simple chapel, listening to the flute and cello music that accompanies the **chazan**, you praise God and give the deepest thanks of your heart that you have been fortunate enough to have had a small role in making this vision come true. You have helped establish a strong link between your beloved adopted country, Israel, and the future leaders of liberal Judaism throughout the world. You have made a difference in the Jewish world of tomorrow, and you are content.

END

55

One of your students has been spending more and more time at an ultra-**Orthodox yeshivah** in **Bnei Brak**. You are not sure what the impact of this training will be on him, but you do not need to wonder for very long. One evening, when one of your adult classes is practicing drawing the figure of a woman, he bursts into the studio. "This is a *chilul HaShem*," he cries out, "an insult to God. Men should never look this way at a woman. It is not right; it is not modest."

With that, he grabs a broom and smashes the sculptures and paintings that are placed around the room. Years of your work and that of your students are ruined in only a few minutes. The studio is in shambles, and students are sitting on the floor, sobbing.

You are not young any more. You have a family and responsibilities, and you wonder if you can muster up the courage and the strength to start all over again. Then, your students turn to you. "We know you survived the *Shoah* and made a new life and family for yourself in Israel. Surely, you can also overcome this setback. We love you. We shall help. Together, we shall begin again. After all, if the Jewish people could wait nineteen centuries between the destruction of the Temple in **Jerusalem** and today's reborn Israel, we can certainly rebuild this school."

With tears in your eyes, you hug them close to you. Their support of what you have tried to do means that your life has been completely worthwhile.

END

56

It is with just this kind of determination that Jews have survived throughout the centuries, and it is, you are quite sure, with the same iron will that your daughter will reach her goal. You and your wife are intensely proud of her. She is a prickly **sabra** of the very best type.

She enters Tel Aviv University and receives a degree in aeronautical engineering. Then, she is admitted to the flight-training program of **El Al**. To no one's surprise, she completes the schooling with the highest of marks and is assigned to be a copilot on flights between **Tel Aviv** and various European capitals.

As you look at this confident and competent young woman in her new blue uniform with the gold stripes on the sleeve, you are content. "As a Jewish man," you think to yourself, "I fought in several wars to protect the Jewish state. I helped build up this nation and the city of **Jerusalem**. Now, my daughter, a Jewish woman, is building up our country in a different way. The planes she flies will bring many people to Israel. Some will stay here and become citizens of this land. Others will go home to tell their friends about our wonderful country. Either way, what she is doing is just as important as anything I ever did. She is truly finishing the work that I began."

END

What they are saying, however, has now become very personal to you. Your daughter has fallen in love with a young man in **England**. As they dated, he went with her to synagogue services and became interested in the Jewish religion for himself. Now he has converted to Judaism under the supervision of the **Reform Synagogue of Great Britain**. But the **Orthodox** rabbis of Israel will not recognize him as a legitimate Jew. A case has been entered in Israel's Supreme Court, and it is likely that they will require the government to register your future son-in-law as a Jew. This enrages the **Orthodox** rabbis.

The National Religious Party and several smaller **Orthodox** political movements decide that it is now time to change the **Law of Return**. "If we can convince the **Knesset** to add the word *k'halachah,* 'according to strict traditional religious law,' to the sentence dealing with conversion, we shall make this *shanda* impossible. Only conversions performed under our direct supervision will be acceptable. The actions of those pseudo-Jews outside of the Holy Land will be forever illegal."

You realize that if their proposal is accepted, your daughter's husband will no longer be considered a Jew. This is serious. This is personal.

If you enter the controversy to protect your family, turn to page 181.

If you reflect on the situation and wonder if, your own situation notwithstanding, they may be right in the long run, turn to page 34.

58

You climb the three flights of stairs to the cramped and cold apartment that the **Jewish Agency for Israel** has assigned to you. You live—yes, it's hard to believe—better than many of the Jews who have grown up in **Rostov**, but the one room is still very small, and you miss your wife and children, who have remained in the **United States**. You know you are doing an important **mitzvah**, but still, in the dark of night, it is lonely.

As you reach your door, you stop suddenly. On the door in red paint is the word *Zhid*, "Jew," and below it a note. You don't need to be a fluent Russian speaker to understand. You are not welcome in **Rostov**. Get out! Or something very bad will happen to you.

Doing a **mitzvah** is one thing, but endangering your life when you have a family is quite another. You pack your few belongings. As it happens, tomorrow morning the weekly **Don Avia** flight from **Rostov** to **Tel Aviv** will depart with many Jews who have decided—often with your help and guidance—that their future will be better in Israel than in southern **Russia**. You will be on that flight.

It is just about two hours in the air. You can see the blue **Mediterranean** below the wing as the airplane banks to the left, and then the coastline, the Land of Israel. When the plane comes to a halt at Ben-Gurion Airport, you descend to a noisy and happy welcome.

And then the biggest surprise of all. Your wife and children stand on the tarmac, arms outstretched to greet you. "We always knew you wanted to return to Israel. And we want to be with you. If this is your homeland, it will be ours, too. *Baruch haba,*" they say in the Hebrew that they have learned at the *ulpan*, "welcome home."

END

59

Almost a hundred years ago, a small band of Jews fled the oppression of the Russian tzars and came to Palestine. There, they established settlements called **kibbutzim** where every member of the group would be treated equally. All property would be owned by the **kibbutz**, not by the members; each person would be given whatever was necessary for his or her needs, but each person would also work as needed to support the **kibbutz**. This kind of collective existence was a wonderful experiment in fair and equal living, and it continues into your own time in Israel's many **kibbutzim**.

There are, of course, many different kinds of **kibbutzim**—**Orthodox**, secular, **socialist** . . . many different kinds. But the discussion of the questions that you and the war veterans have been wrestling with seems most active in a new settlement in the **Arava**, that wide valley that runs from the southern end of the **Dead Sea** to the **Gulf of Aqaba**. This **kibbutz** is named **Lotan**, and it was founded by young **Reform** Jewish immigrants from the **United States** and other western countries.

Perhaps because they have moved to Israel in search of a meaningful Jewish life, the residents of **Lotan** are intensely interested in the questions the veterans have asked. These young people welcome you into their midst. "Stay with us," they say. "Help lead discussions with us about peace and meaning and why things happen the way they do and so on. That will be an important contribution to our life."

No choice, you think, could have been better. To be surrounded by young, interesting people who want to learn from you—that's the best! You are a very happy person.

END

60

Like **Abraham** before you, you climb to the top of a low hill and look out over the desert landscape. On one side of the little road that winds its way through the rocky scene, the land is brown and barren. Nothing grows there. But on the other side, your side, the land is green and productive.

Your mind is alive with thoughts, and somehow, you get an image of a **Chanukah dreidel**. "Why," you wonder, "would I ever think of that at this very moment? What do you suppose brought that vision to my mind?" Then the answer flashes clearly. On the sides of the little top are four Hebrew letters— *nun, gimel, hei, pei*—and each letter stands for the first letter of a Hebrew word—*neis gadol hayah po,* "a great miracle has happened here."

Like the **Maccabees** of old, you went to war against a powerful enemy. But this enemy was not an army of men and horses; it was the enemy of desert lands and hungry people. And you have prevailed! You have emerged from this conflict victorious. With your help, starving men and women and children can eat food; they will be able to live.

This legacy of bringing the desert land back to life reminds you once again of the promise of **Pesach**. "Let all who are hungry come and eat." You are certain that when they come, you and many others have now found a way to grow food to fill their stomachs. You have performed a very important **mitzvah**, and you are content.

END

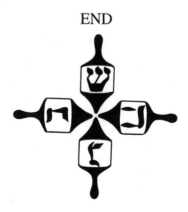

61

For one thing, you do not know any Arabic. How can you live and work among people who speak this language without knowing it yourself? You know Polish, **Yiddish**, Hebrew, and a smattering of other languages, but very little Arabic. This is a lack you've got to remedy. You enroll in an Arabic language program at the **Hebrew University** on **Mount Scopus** in **Jerusalem** and begin your study.

Modern Arabic, you find, is easy for you to learn. Many of the words sound like Hebrew, and soon you can speak rather fluently. But the big surprise for you is yet to come. You take a course in medieval Arabic poetry, and you fall in love with the beauty and grace of this literature. Very soon, you understand why **Moses Maimonides**, the greatest Jewish philosopher of all times, wrote his most important work, *The Guide for the Perplexed*, in Arabic. This discovery makes you feel like you have come around a turn in a mountain path and now stand face-to-face with the most gorgeous scenery you could ever imagine. You want the image of this beauty in your life for the rest of your days.

You finish your studies at the university and are offered a teaching position. Without hesitation, you accept and spend the rest of your days helping students come to an appreciation of this ancient language. To have lived in the Jewish state, but with the rhythms of medieval Arabic poetry in your mind and on your tongue, makes your life complete. You live out the rest of your life as a fully contented person.

END

62

What a strange group of men stand at the door of your office! Each of them is dressed in a floor-length, hooded, brown garment. A rope belt is tied around the waist, and their hands are concealed in the full, flowing sleeves. A short, balding man at the front of the group addresses you. "We are monks from the Carmelite monastery in **Haifa**. One of our members very much needs your legal help."

You invite them to sit down. "Please tell me about his situation."

"Our Brother Daniel was born a Jew in **Poland** in the early 1920s. When the **Nazis** conquered his country in 1940, he was able to get a job in **Gestapo** headquarters. You can imagine how dangerous that must have been for him. But, with great courage, he was able to pass information about raids to Jewish communities. Not many lives were saved in the long run, but he tried desperately to help his fellow Jews. Finally, the Germans realized that there was a spy among them. Brother Daniel (his family name was then Oswald) fled to a Carmelite monastery, which was glad to hide him. He converted to the Catholic religion, originally to protect himself, and he survived the war. Now, he lives in our community in **Haifa**, and he has applied for Israeli citizenship under the **Law of Return**. We want you to plead his case and help him become an Israeli citizen."

You ask for a day or two to think about this case. It is unusual. Is Brother Daniel a Jew because he was born of a Jewish mother? Or is he a Catholic because he converted?

To continue your research and thinking, turn to page 30.

If you wonder what caused Brother Daniel to abandon Judaism, turn to page 156.

63

Building an archaeological research school in **Jerusalem** is not as easy as it sounds. **Orthodox** groups strongly oppose the creation of an institution that will be allied with American **Reform Judaism.** "It's a *chilul HaShem!*" they exclaim. "What an insult to God and to real Judaism. **Reform** is not even Judaism; it's a form of idolatry."

With great courage, **Glueck**'s friend, **Teddy Kollek**, resists these pressures. He makes available to this visionary leader a piece of ground on **King David Street**, a plot from which you can even see across the **Green Line** to the walls of the **Old City**. It is a magnificent location, and even you can visualize the new school and its potential on this site.

As the workmen begin to raise the walls of the academy, a new threat appears. **Chasidic** Jews, young men in black coats and hats, gather in the street. They throw stones at this hated symbol of modern Jewish life, a style of life that differs so radically from their own. And at night some of them try to sneak onto the property and destroy what the workers had erected during the day. Against his will, **Glueck** is forced to hire armed guards. "Try not to shoot anyone," he cautions. "But do keep them off our grounds. We have a right to build the school of which we dream."

When the first archaeology students arrive at the completed campus, you turn to **Dr. Glueck.** "Well, you've accomplished your goal. You have finished the project. Aren't you proud!" But he looks at you with a little smile. "You think we are finished? Wrong! Archaeology not only lets me look into the past. I can also see the future. And we have a long way to go before this project is done."

*To see what **Glueck** sees in the future, turn to page 54.*

64

Israel's Supreme Court rules against Brother Daniel, and you concur. It's probably the right decision, but you still want to do something to support his claim to Israeli citizenship. What can you do?

In a moment of insight, you figure out the solution. You write a letter to Brother Daniel, offering to sponsor him in his application for citizenship. The process of becoming an Israeli through naturalization is slower, but it is open to anyone who wishes, including, of course, Brother Daniel. Helping him in this way, you think, is the least you could do after the risks he took. For all you know, information that he relayed out of **Gestapo** headquarters in **Warsaw** might have saved your own life.

A little to your surprise, he accepts your offer. The wheels of the Israeli government grind very slowly, but five years later, you and Brother Daniel are summoned to court. "Who is the sponsor of this man?" the judge asks. "I am, sir. I am very proud to serve as his sponsor and witness as he becomes a citizen of our country." Brother Daniel raises his hand and, in fluent Hebrew, takes the oath of citizenship.

"Now," you say as you turn to shake his hand, "there is only one law for us, one law for the native-born Jew and the convert. Now, we are both under the same roof after a very long time. *Mazal tov!*"

END

65

You are outraged that Israel might give **Taba** back to the Egyptians. This is an area you have been using for your tourist business. It's not fair. It's not right. That your own government could destroy all your efforts in this way makes you furious. But how can one simple citizen resist? You've been undermined and damaged, but what can you do? And if it's in the cause of peace, maybe it's the right thing to do after all, even if it's bad for you personally.

You sell your hotel and dive boat and move back to **Tel Aviv**. Actually, not to **Tel Aviv** itself, but to a town a few miles to its southeast named **Rishon LeZion**. One of the first settlements of Russian Jews in Palestine after the oppression of 1881–1882, **Rishon LeZion** is about as much a part of Israel as anywhere. No one would ever dream of giving it back to the Arabs!

You were displaced from your home in Europe. Then, you had to move from the **displaced persons' camp** to Palestine. In Israel, you first lived in **Jerusalem**, then **Jaffa**, then **Eilat**. Finally, even the Israeli government has forced you to relocate again.

Now, you have found the one place from which you will never again be required to move. You may need to drive into **Tel Aviv**, that growing city where there will certainly be jobs for you to take, but your home in **Rishon LeZion** will always be part of Israel. With that assurance, you can safely live out your days without any worry.

END

66

The small factory for logic boards that you have started in an unused barn is successful. If it is to continue, it needs to expand. Bigger will be better, you are certain. Now it is time to put into action the secret long-range plan that you had in your mind from the very beginning.

Just before lunch one day, you stand at the door of the factory's office as a caravan of large cars arrives. Young men and women from several of Israel's cities step out of these fancy vehicles. These are not at all like the tractors that used to drive up and down the dirt roads of the farm, and these young people look very different from the settlers in their floppy blue hats and baggy pants. You wonder if any of them have ever used a shovel or a hoe. Would they even know what one is?

You've invited these people to your community because they recognize two things that are important in the modern world: they understand hi-tech industry, and they understand money and investments. After lunch, you take them on a tour of your factory, and they are impressed. This may not be the "good old days," but you and your workers have created a second miracle. First, you were able to convert bare land into a very successful farm; now you have turned that farm into a small factory.

Before they leave, these investors agree to finance an expansion. "This place will be one of the centers of Israel's growing computer industry. We can visualize buildings full of highly skilled, intelligent workers leading our nation into the twenty-first century. And it won't hurt that all of us will make a lot of money along the way!"

To follow the growth of this industrial expansion, turn to page 72.

67

After the **War of Independence**, the situation of Jews living in Arab lands became increasingly difficult. From **Morocco, Algeria,** and **Tunisia**, some migrated to **France**, and others went to other lands. But most of them turned toward the east and left for Israel. "After all," they said, "for years we have prayed for a return to the holy land of **Zion**. Now we must do that. Israel will be our new homeland."

You notice that some of their children, especially the youngsters from families from **Yemen**, have a real talent for art. You begin to give art classes in their schools, teaching them how to draw and paint and mold blocks of clay into stylish figures. Within a short time, some of these young people begin to hang around your **Jaffa** gallery. They are full of curiosity; question after question pours from their mouths as they ask about your work.

Your young daughter gives you an idea. "*Abba,*" she says, "why don't you start a school for these children? It would be a shame if their interest and talent had no way to grow and develop." She's absolutely right, and you do exactly that. Soon, your afternoon classes are full of happy, active children. Some of them are really quite good, and you can see that they may have careers in art ahead of them.

After fifteen years of art classes, you are faced with a surprise. If you want to know what it is, turn to page 53.

If, on the other hand, you are shocked when one of your students takes a destructive path, turn to page 55.

68

Your own son, now in his twenties, befriends this teenage rebel. They often go camping together, and during one trip to the **Negev** they spend the night near some **Bedouin** tents. At dawn, your son looks for his companion, but he is no longer curled up in his sleeping bag. Instead, he is sitting on a rocky hill, watching the **Bedouins** as their day begins. He is fascinated by the men shepherding the goats, sheep, and camels; by the women and children starting fires, cooking **pita** bread, boiling water for extra-strong coffee. "I've never seen anything like this anywhere," he shouts. "This is amazing. It's almost like I am watching people from biblical times—but they are living right now."

Eventually, your son pries him off his rock, and the two of them load their gear into the little car you let them borrow on weekends. They drive north, into the desert capital city of **Beersheba**, where your son parks the car. "I want you to meet a friend of our family. He is a professor of anthropology at the **Ben-Gurion University of the Negev**. He spends all his time studying the **Bedouin** people you have been observing."

And so it is that this young man's life is changed. The professor's passion for his studies and the teenager's excitement merge; he is now captured by the life of the mind, and amassing things no longer means much to him. What a transformation! You know now that he will spend the rest of his life in the pursuit of knowledge, and you are ever grateful to your own son, who gave him this opportunity for hope.

END

69

You work hard in your adopted city of **Haifa**, establishing programs that bring youth of different backgrounds together. It's been hard and challenging at times, but also rewarding. One day you need a break, so you go for a ride. The hill rises sharply, almost bursting from the blue waters of the **Mediterranean Sea**. There is a narrow flat plateau at its base, then a rapid ascent to another modest pause in the middle, then another climb to the summit. **Mount Carmel**, the hill on which the city of **Haifa** is taking shape, is, indeed, a biblical mountain. It was here that the **prophet Elijah** engaged the **prophet**s of the idol **Baal** in a contest; it was here that he proved that the God of Israel is the true and only God.

Today, **Haifa** is home to Jewish descendants of **Elijah** and the ancient Israelites, but also to Christians, **Moslems**, and **Baha'is**. To be sure, there are neighborhoods where more of one group lives than another, but the city itself is a jumble of races and religions. If people of different backgrounds can ever manage to live together, it ought to happen in **Haifa**. So, it is here that you settle, right on top of **Elijah**'s mountain, to see if you can help cause understanding to flourish among these many peoples.

Decades of dedicated work pass, but you dare not claim that true friendship exists. Yet you are quite sure that your work has helped **Haifa** remain at peace while other cities in Israel have been torn by conflicts between Jews and **Moslems**, Israelis and Arabs. No doubt, you have contributed a great deal to the welfare of this beautiful city and, while true *shalom*, the ideal of your life, still lies in the future, you know that you have helped a place where different people can, at least, live next to each other without fear. To have achieved even this much means that your life's work has been worthwhile.

END

70

Just north of the Palestinian Arab town of **Gaza** is the Israeli city of **Ashkelon**. It was in this region that biblical Israel's enemies, the **Philistines**, lived, and it seems that little has changed in three thousand years. Israel's most angry opponents walk the dusty streets of **Gaza** and gather in its cafes to exchange complaints about the Jewish state. It is in **Gaza** that attacks across the border are often planned.

With the help of the Israeli government, you transform a large section of land into a farm. You plant a particular kind of onion that has always grown in this region and even got its name from the city—scallions. Agriculture requires lots of workers, so you can offer jobs to a number of the young men who live in **Gaza**. While they work in your fields, you will be able to listen to them and overhear the plans they share. (They do not realize you speak Arabic, and you are not about to tell them.)

Of course, you are only partly a farmer; in truth, you are an agent of the Israeli intelligence service, gathering information on **Hezbollah** and **Fatah** groups that seek to gain power among these unhappy youth. Israel must know what plans they are making, and the unguarded conversations of these agricultural workers may just provide the information that will protect Israelis and the State of Israel.

You spend the rest of your life digging up stinky onions and uncovering bad-smelling pieces of information. But the results seem awfully good to you.

END

71

You don't like what you hear. When the **Nazis** came to power in **Germany**, you heard similar remarks, then too about Jews. To be sure, many things were different, but the slurs were still about Jews. And the prejudice of those remarks was carefully concealed in coded expressions—"We just don't want foreigners in our country"—just like the comments about these Black Jews in **Dimona**. "I've learned through painful experience that prejudice and discrimination can begin with subtle hatred. But look where it ended up. With the murder of six million Jews. The only place to stop these hateful attitudes and remarks is right at the beginning."

If you are going to change the attitudes of the residents of **Dimona**, you have work to do right here, right at home, right next door. The people you have to change are the same people who shop in stores with you, whose children go to school with your children and kick soccer balls with them on the athletic fields. They are not monsters or evil people, but somehow you have to teach them that prejudice, like a disease, can be contagious. And once it starts to spread, controlling it gets more and more difficult.

This is a serious, major commitment. If you are going to undertake this goal, you need to live in or near **Dimona**. But you also need to illustrate your own values by how you live your life. You cannot allow anyone to accuse you of being a phony, of being a hypocrite. You must find a place to live that is close but that also shows by its daily life the values you want to teach. Such places are not easy to find.

But you do locate one **kibbutz** that qualifies. When you describe your ambition to its leaders, they invite you to move to the **kibbutz** and use it as the base of your operations.

To do so, turn to page 42.

72

When the **kibbutz** was new and agriculture was the main occupation, many young people became bored. They would go into the military for their required service and then move to the city; few of them returned to the **kibbutz** and its collective way of life. Over glasses of tea in the evening, you and some of the old-timers wondered if you would be able to keep the settlement alive if the younger generation continued leaving.

Now, however, you are all in the midst of a hi-tech revolution. People from the cities, especially really sharp and interesting young men and women, are coming to live in the area, and your own young people are deciding to stay and make their future here. You walk around from one factory to the next, smiling all the time. This was your secret plan all along. It had nothing to do with industry, but with creating conditions that would be attractive to young adults. By changing the nature of the **kibbutz**, you have made it a place where a new group of young people wants to come, and that has guaranteed the future.

"We started growing one kind of plant, and that worked for a while. But the world changes, and we had to change with it. Now, we are growing a different kind of plants . . . industrial plants. Our future grows better with them. It's just like the **prophet** said: 'Not by might nor by power, but by My spirit shall all men live in peace.' We shall live in peace because we have used the spirit of the intelligence and brains that God has given us to make this miracle happen."

END

73

The silver jewelry these men make is really wonderful. Yet you are convinced that the future of Israel lies in technology. You convince them to find jobs making computers and building sophisticated airplanes. They can always continue their jewelry craft in the evenings, after work.

Capable and intelligent, these workers learn their new jobs quickly and become highly valued employees. Their bosses frequently tell you that they could not operate their factories without such workers.

To your surprise, however, they learn another skill as well . . . how to strike. While you were not paying attention, organizers from the Histadrut, Israel's General Federation of Labor, had been meeting with the workers, providing additional education and guidance, teaching them how to improve their pay and working conditions by banding together.

Now, with the help of the Histadrut, the workers meet with their employers. "We think we are worth more than you are paying us. If you do not give us more money, we simply will not continue; we shall go out on strike," they say. "It's not a solution we want, and we are pretty sure you don't want that either. So let's get together and work out a deal."

If the companies offer a raise, but it may not be enough, turn to page 162.

If one of the workers realizes that the problem is bigger than one or two companies and sets out to deal with the larger picture, turn to page 125.

74

Toward the northeastern corner of the **Negev**, construction has begun on the new city of **Dimona**. From the arid, inhospitable land, a city welcomes home tens of thousands of new residents. Schools and community centers and shops—all the necessities of urban life grow as if stimulated to grow by the bright sunshine.

Another group of new residents takes up housing in this development town. They are not like the immigrant settlers. Instead, they are very well educated and keep mostly to themselves. If someone asks what they do, they change the subject or walk away. "Who," you wonder, "are these Israelis who want little to do with their neighbors?"

Every morning, they board special buses and drive to a construction site outside the city. A tall fence guards their workplace, and armed patrols stand at every gate. Rumors fly in every direction. "They're designing new airplanes." "They are working with dangerous chemicals." You've even heard that they are breeding kosher pigs! Soon, however, the truth slips out. **Dimona** will be the site of Israel's only nuclear reactor. Inside the fence, these scientists will produce energy that could power the country or produce an atomic bomb. What goes on inside the fence is top, top secret, but everybody knows anyway.

The power plant breeds more than nuclear energy. Everyone is on the lookout for enemies and spies. It seems that protecting Israel leads to defensiveness and suspicion. It's hard to know whom you can trust.

If a group of immigrants arrive who raise your concern, turn to page 16.

If a controversy about Israel's atomic bomb explodes, turn to page 155.

75

Disguised as an old Arab woman, you lead a donkey up the hill, away from the beach, toward **Jerusalem**. It will not be easy to bypass the British army's patrols, but somehow you manage, and after ten days of walking, you enter the city. You are so exhausted that you cannot imagine how you will move even one step further. But you do. The drive for survival is like that; it calls up from within you unexpected energy.

An old Arab man appears next to you and quietly says, "Follow me, but stay two steps behind me." (You would not understand him in Arabic, but, to your surprise, he speaks **Yiddish**.) Like a dutiful Arab wife, you walk in his tracks until you reach a small stone house. Then he takes the donkey from you and motions you inside.

Finally, you are able to strip off your dusty clothing and wash the dark-colored makeup off your face. The trick worked, and now you can hide safely in this house, which belongs to members of the **Haganah**. You stay there until May 14, 1948, when you and thousands of other Jewish residents of the city gather to hear **David Ben-Gurion** read the Declaration of Independence of the State of Israel aloud for the first time. Goose bumps cover your arms as you realize that you are a witness to history. For the first time in nineteen hundred years, Jews have a land of their own.

*If you decide to enlist in the **Palmach** and volunteer for combat, turn to page 129.*

*If you think your talents might be more useful as a training officer in the **Haganah**, turn to page 93.*

76

Your daughter discovers that it is forbidden to dig in certain areas near the **Temple Mount**. "There might be a cemetery there," she is told, "and we do not permit anyone to disturb even an ancient Jewish grave." The man who speaks to her is intense and earnest. He stares through shining black eyes, eyes surrounded by dark brows and an even darker beard. "We are among the faithful of the **Temple Mount**. Soon, *Moshiach* will come, and we shall rebuild the Temple, just as it was in biblical times. We are ready. We actually have fashioned all the tools of the Sanctuary. All we need is *Moshiach,* the Messiah, and we can begin immediately."

Rebuilding the ancient Temple and sacrificing animals strike her as strange ideas, but she is not ready to argue with him. He looks like he won't be persuaded by any words or ideas; he has already made up his mind. So she moves her dig farther south, just to the west of the great steps that lead up to the Temple's wall and gate. This was possibly the site of the original City of David.

She and her crew dig a trench through the dirt and rubble. As she steps back from the work, she can see the different layers of dirt, each a different color, each containing evidence from a different historical period. One of the layers is dark gray, not brown. Embedded in it is a triangular stone. When she digs it out, it has a Hebrew inscription: *LASHOFAR,* "for the shofar blower." It must have come from the **Second Temple**, which was destroyed by the Romans in 70 C.E. This is a really exciting find.

If you stand with your daughter at the edge of her dig and think serious thoughts, turn to page 9.

If you do something that almost causes you to have a serious problem at the dig, turn to page 152.

The Ministry of Agriculture agrees to let you try an experiment. "But," they warn you, "the test must be serious and hard. Otherwise, you won't prove anything important. Take some ground near the biblical city of **Sodom**, down by the south end of the **Dead Sea**. That's about the worst soil in all of Israel. If you can make that area bloom, you will have proved your point."

They are right. This soil is dry and rocky and, more than anything else, full of chemical salts, like chlorine and bromine. Nothing lives in the **Dead Sea**—that's why they call it "dead"— and nothing would ever grow in this awful dirt. Still, if you can make this land bear crops, you can do it anywhere.

The first challenge, the thing you've got to do before any other step, is to figure out how to get these chemicals out of the soil. Unless you can remove them, your test will certainly fail. You convince the Water Authority to let you use some of the precious water from the **Jordan River** to wash the salts out of one small acre of land. "If it works with that water, we can always pump water from the sea near **Eilat** and remove the salt from that ocean water. It may not be good enough to drink, but it would be clean enough to wash the soil."

Slowly, you and your assistants direct streams of water at the rocky soil. Fresh water floods the land and then disappears below the surface. Every so often, you test the salt content of the soil, and you are pleased when the tests show that it is greatly reduced. The water keeps flowing until you are satisfied that you have removed enough chemicals to make the land capable of growing a crop.

Now you are ready to take the next step. Turn to page 37.

78

You pull back the mosquito netting that envelops your bed and step outside the hut where you have been staying. It's already been a few months since you arrived in **Chad**, but the results of your efforts are already apparent. The village leaders have gathered a crew of intelligent and vigorous men who are able to follow your teaching and who understand what you tell them. They will certainly be able to keep this project alive once you are back in Israel.

As you button your shirt, you look at the calendar that you have tacked to the wall. Whoa! This is not just any day in October. You look again. Today is **Yom Kippur**. Of course, out here in the dry desert, it's hard to tell one day from the next, so you may be forgiven for not realizing that the **High Holy Days** were upon you.

For a few moments, you feel guilty and ashamed. You should have been in the synagogue at home, praying with your family and friends. That's where they are now, so there is no use trying to call them. But this evening you will. The **High Holy Days** simply are not the same if you aren't with your family.

Then, a wave of excitement sweeps over you. Right about now, the cantor must be chanting the **haftarah** from **Isaiah** [58:7]. That ancient prophet wrote that the real fast that God wants is for you to distribute your bread to the hungry, and here you are, right on **Yom Kippur**, fulfilling the most basic **mitzvah** of the Bible. Right then, you feel a burden of sadness lifted from your shoulders. It doesn't seem so bad to be separated from your family now, knowing that you are doing exactly what God wants from you.

END

79

When you return to Israel, a group of farmers from **Chad** accompanies you. They have already learned the basics of drip irrigation, but there is so much more about scientific farming that you can teach them. And they are eager to learn, because they know firsthand the horror of watching people starve to death.

What a strange scene this must be to someone who does not know the story! A group of very black African men, gathered at a farm in Israel, pausing at the beginning of their meals while you and your Israeli friends chant *HaMotzi,* then moving to the room you have set aside for them to kneel on their prayer rugs and praise *Allah.* Middle Eastern Jews and African **Moslems**, here together with the common purpose of feeding the hungry of their nation. You know that there is enough hatred in the world for everyone, but here, at least for this little space in time, all of you are friends.

As they finish their classes and prepare to head back to **Chad**, all of you gather for a final meal together. With wine for you and juice for these **Moslems** who do not drink alcohol, you raise your glasses in a toast. They already know the correct Hebrew word to use—*l'chayim,* "to life." Together, you are able to celebrate life, for it is indeed life that you have all made possible through the miracle of bringing growth and food to the desert. You put your arms around your wife and children. "I know it was hard when I was away. But look at these men. They will embrace their families tomorrow . . . and for many tomorrows after that, because their families will live. I have been a partner with God in bringing life to their villages. What else could be so rewarding or important?"

END

80

You march up and down outside the Ministry of Justice in **Jerusalem** carrying a protest sign. "No more bombs," your placard reads. "Release the man who spoke the truth."

Other protesters hold signs for a different point of view, but you are convinced that Israel does not need atomic bombs to protect itself. "Listen," you say. "If we have the bomb, then other nations will want one too. Already **India** and **Pakistan** are working on atomic weapons. We know **Iraq** is moving in that direction, and soon other countries will too. It won't be very long before some terrorist organization finds a way to acquire one. Then, there will be no limits. Some idiot will use one of these bombs, and then our entire planet will go up in smoke. There must be a way to stop the spread of weapons that can destroy so many lives. The safest thing for Israel and for all the nations of the world is to ban all nuclear weapons. Our world and our country would be much more secure if no one had an atomic bomb."

You know in your heart that there must be another way to defend Israel. Atomic warfare will not save your country; it will only cause millions of people to die and provoke other countries to explode their own bombs. If it is the last thing you do in your life, you will find that other way. "Let them learn war no more" [Isaiah 2:4], you chant, as you stride firmly around the circle of protesters. You will do whatever it takes to move Israel and the rest of the nations of the world toward nuclear disarmament.

END

81

Many of the immigrants feel comfortable in **Beersheba**, the capital city of the **Negev**. Camels and donkeys wander through the streets, while Jews and **Bedouin** Arabs mingle in the *shuk*. It is an exciting city, so full of energy and activity that it is hard to keep your mind on the basic Hebrew lessons that you teach these immigrants. The men, at least, know the Hebrew of the *siddur,* but prayer-book Hebrew won't get them very far when they try to buy lunch at the corner **falafel** stand. They've got to learn the modern language of this modern country. And so do you! As an immigrant who arrived just a year or so before these people, you have to study long hours every night, just to keep ahead of them in class. In the adventure of settling into Israel, you are all learning together.

One day, you notice that one of the younger men is sketching something on a pad during class. Your first thought is to scold him and to tell him to pay attention. But your eye is drawn to his design. It is complex and beautiful, a woman's brooch with a delicate filigree design. After class, you ask to see the picture. "This is beautiful. Have you made other patterns like this one?" "Of course I have! Many of the men from our country of **Yemen** are skilled silversmiths. One of our traditional occupations was to make jewelry."

You encourage some of the men to open a small jewelry workshop, and their products quickly become very popular. Some of them are quite smart. They ought to go to the university. To help them do so, turn to page 23.

You also try to convince some of them to gain other skills. To move in this direction, turn to page 73.

82

Despite your disappointment at **Zohar**, you have not completely lost your idealism. You still believe that living in harmony with others must be possible and that collective settlements are the way to accomplish that aim. You move to a new Israeli settlement, just north of the town of **El Al** in the recently captured **Golan Heights**. You are particularly fond of this location because on **Shabbat** you and your family can walk a few miles to the biblical **Yarmuk River** and retell the stories of **Jacob and Esau**.

Apple trees and grape vines—this new settlement is experimenting with the growing of fruit as its main industry. You have no experience in agriculture, but you are pretty good at business, so they assign you to the sales office. With your staff, you design an attractive showroom where busloads of tourists can come, taste the wine that your neighbors produce, and, you hope, buy some of the bottles. More than that, you hope they will carry the news of Israel's new product to their homes. You even come up with a catchy slogan: "Drink Golan wine. It's for more than just *Kiddush!*"

As the tourists stand around sipping your wine, you have a chance to explain to them the special qualities of this area of Israel—its climate, the people who have moved here, its importance in defending Israel from Syrian gunners, the archaeological finds that have begun to turn up. After a few years, the Prime Minister of Israel visits your showroom. He has a special surprise for you. "I hereby give you the title of 'Ambassador of the **Golan**.' I wish Israel had more spokesmen like you. *Mazal tov!*"

END

83

Walking along **King David Street** in **Jerusalem**, you notice a class of schoolchildren with their teacher. They have stopped in front of a small stone sculpture. The students gently place their hands on the cold stone, feeling its curves and texture. You can hear them talking about what the artist tried to say with this work, and you are impressed. How wonderful it must be to move a group of youngsters with a work of art!

You are so affected by this event that you enroll in the **Bezalel** School of Art and spend the next several years learning how to be a sculptor. But you prefer working with metal rather than chiseling on stone. One of your works, a very large piece about the prophet **Isaiah**, is purchased by the city of **Jerusalem** and installed in a park not far from where you had first seen the young people admiring the stone piece.

But **Jerusalem** is not the place where you want to live or work. You need to be among other artists, so you buy a small house in the old Arab city of **Jaffa**, a southern suburb of **Tel Aviv**. It is here that an artist colony is developing, here that people who want to buy works of art come to tour the galleries, here that you will open your own showroom. To your surprise, art patrons and tourists flock to this section of the city. Your bank account swells with their money. What a pleasant surprise!

There are two more surprises in your future. Two new opportunities to use your artistic talent are presented to you.

One involves the Shalom, *a new ship of the Israeli Zim line. If you agree to help decorate her staterooms and public spaces,* *turn to page 103.*

A new Israeli tourist center is being planned for the area of **Eilat**. *If you consent to work on this development,* *turn to page 182.*

84

Orthodox Jews, you are sure, are not all identical. There are some who are very rigid and firm, others who are more flexible, even in Israel. You share your problem with an old friend, and he says he has just the answer. "I know a rabbi in **Kiryat Shemona** who is **Orthodox**. He follows the **halachah**, but with a human face. If you come up to the town, I'll make the connection. I am pretty sure that everything will be all right."

He seems so sure. It's worth a try, although it takes a little convincing to get your future son-in-law to agree. After all, he has been hurt before, and he does not want to go through this pain again. Still, you all climb into the car one morning and drive all the way up to the northern end of the **Galilee**.

Ten years later, as you walk your little grandson home from his *cheder,* you know that all of you were right to take the chance. Your son-in-law *davens* every morning in a traditional *shul.* He enjoys praying with his friends, and sometimes you too join them for *Shacharit,* the morning prayers. Your daughter has made good friends with the other women of the synagogue; most of their social life is centered around this synagogue and the lives of the families who pray there.

The kindly rabbi of **Kiryat Shemona** died a few years ago, but every year on his *yahrzeit* you go to the cemetery and leave a little pebble on his marker. It is the least you can do to remember this man; after all, God blessed you in many ways through him.

END

85

The war is finally over, and Israel's independence is assured. But you are strangely uneasy about yourself. The country may be independent, but you feel that you are still a prisoner of your feelings, feelings about what happened to you and your family under the **Nazis** in Europe. You will not truly be able to fulfill yourself until you have taken care of those emotions. But how? As you think about them, they are intense and strong and very confusing. What to do?

Some survivors deal with their feelings by refusing to talk about the *Shoah*, but you are aware enough of yourself to know that this will not work for you. You must confront the emotions directly. And that means placing yourself in contact with German citizens, people who were involved themselves in World War II or whose families were.

This is difficult. But you create a program that invites Germans to come to Israel as tourists and as temporary workers on the **kibbutzim**. "We can certainly use their help," you tell people who are not sure about this program, "and, perhaps, while they are here, we can start to build bridges of understanding and reconciliation. It's worth a try."

When you and your wife have children, you raise them with the same values. Your son goes on to establish a program called **Neve Shalom/Wahat al-Salaam**, a village in which Israeli Jews and Arabs live, work, and study together, striving for peace and greater understanding.

If your daughter does not agree with your approach and takes another direction, turn to page 171.

If a visitor has a strange impact on her, turn to page 107.

86

"Once you were famous; now you are a simple worker. Moving to Israel has been a disaster for you. In the former **Soviet Union**, at least, you were somebody important. I am ashamed of you here." His son blurts out these angry words, then rushes out of the apartment and slams the door. You wish you could reason with him, explain that his father willingly changed his life so that he could live in freedom as a Jew without the threat of anti-Semitism. But he won't listen.

He stops going to his high school classes and begins to hang out with a group of former Russian kids. You don't know what they do when they are together, but you are suspicious. They look more and more like a gang of young toughs and trouble-makers.

One day in May, help comes from two unexpected sources. One of his friends, Anatoly, is caught by the police selling drugs. He is arrested and taken to jail. In shock, he admits, "I really didn't believe that this would happen. We were just angry kids. But drugs . . . that's a different story." And, while he is telling you this tale—and you believe him when he says he is surprised—the postman brings an envelope for him. It is from the Ministry of Defense, informing him that he must report for military duty in July.

A year later, when he hitchhikes home for **Shabbat**, you look at a different young man. He is now muscular and tanned. He stands straight with a posture of self-confidence. Tzahal, the Israeli army, has made him into a proud Israeli. He has even come to understand the sacrifices his father made to give him a chance at a new kind of life. *"Baruch shegmalani kol tov,"* you say, "Praised be God, who eventually did so much good for this boy and his family. Amen."

END

87

An organization called Interns for Peace (IFP) helps Israelis and Palestinians work together. They try to convince ordinary people that they do not have to hate one another. Peace on a piece of paper will not mean much, the founders of IFP say, if the men and women of these two cultures cannot learn to handle their differences without fighting. "We probably won't agree on many things. Maybe we won't even like each other. But there has to be a way to get along without killing each other."

You and your daughter become organizers for IFP. You use all the skills that you gained in the army to train Israelis and Palestinians to work together. One of the ways you hope these different groups will come to trust each other a little is through a survival course. Groups of Palestinian and Israeli young people build the obstacle course that you have designed. They raise a high tower with ropes for climbing, a long log for balancing on, a maze of ropes and stakes that the participant must figure out, and a number of other challenges. None of the obstacles can be completed successfully without help. You think that having Israelis help Palestinians, and Palestinians help Israelis will enable them to succeed in overcoming the biggest obstacles of all: lack of trust and not being able to think of the other person as a human being with feelings and ideas.

The survival course works out beautifully. The young women and men who complete it are proud of their achievement and how they worked together. They have learned a valuable lesson, and now they are ready to share it with others; they are ready to learn how to become workers for peace in their local communities.

*If you take some of them to the **Golan**, turn to page 108.*

*If your daughter takes some of the women to **Gaza**, turn to page 132.*

88

To find a new place to live, you decide to join a tour group on a bus trip through the north of Israel. That way, you will see a great many places very quickly, and you can narrow down your choices to just a few places. The new development towns of **Metulla** and **Kiryat Shemona** hold some interest for you, but not for long. The bus stops at a place called **Dan**. The guide leads your group on a stroll through a darkly shaded grove of trees. The tall greenery forms an arch over the path, and you hear a rushing sound in the distance. Suddenly, you come upon the gushing source of a river. The water is clear and cold. This is a magnificent place. You must live near here.

After you move north, you meet another concentration camp survivor, a woman from **Hungary**. Though the two of you are older than many couples, you decide to marry and start a family as soon as possible. "The **Nazis** took a million and a half children from us. It will be our **mitzvah** to replace a few of them." Your daughter and then your son are born in the hospital near **Dan**, and they grow up to be fine young people.

One **Shabbat** afternoon, you and your family are wandering through your favorite place, the shady grove of trees and the bubbling water source. Your son picks up stones and throws them into the water. Then he stops abruptly. "Look at this stone, *Ima*," he cries out. "*Abba*, there is something scratched on the side of this rock. Do you suppose it could be writing, maybe some ancient message, maybe even from the time of the Bible?"

You don't know anything about ancient writing, but it certainly looks like someone carved shapes into the stone with a purpose. You put the stone in your pocket and promise your family that you will find out what these shapes are as soon as possible.

To find out what you discover, turn to page 52.

89

The more you talk to the friends of the dead shooter, the less you can accept their path to peace. "Peace cannot come," you tell them, "when you murder other people, when you force them from their homes, when you make it impossible for them to earn a decent living. No, this is not the way to make peace."

But they do not agree with you. "There can be no peace with these Arabs if peace means we have to live together. The only way they understand is the way of force. Do you not understand that they want to kill us? We must be able to defend ourselves, and defending ourselves means making them leave our Promised Land."

There can be no compromise between fanatics like these people and the equally determined Arabs of the other side. Maybe they are really right after all. Perhaps the only way to avoid another all-out war is to separate the two sides. If you are really to be a *rodeif shalom,* a person determined to pursue peace, it seems you must find a way to protect the rights of both the settlers and the Arabs, yet also keep them apart. This will not be an easy task.

If you believe that you can only think of solutions when you and your family are living in a place that is completely secure, turn to page 19.

*If you think that you can make more of a difference by running for a seat in the **Knesset**, turn to page 8.*

90

The entire family crowds into the car for the trip to the north of Israel. Your path takes you up the **Mediterranean** coast road, then inland, across the fertile **Jezreel Valley** until you see the shore of the **Kinneret, the Sea of Galilee**. Then, up the shore until you come to the city of **Tiberias**. Your son-in-law pulls the car into a downtown parking place and says, "Everybody out." You and your wife, your daughter and her husband, and your three-year-old grandson all unwind from this long journey and march single file up a hilly sidewalk until you reach a fenced-in area.

"Look, *Ima*," your daughter exclaims. "This is the grave of the **Rambam, Moses Maimonides**, the greatest Jewish scholar who ever lived. This is a very holy place. We shall go in and pray, and then we shall leave a good sum of *tzedakah* with the rabbi who tends this site."

Her excitement and religious passion at this shrine astound you. You have never seen your daughter act like this before, but, apparently, she has become very **Orthodox**. This kind of Judaism is now vitally important to her. But the stop in **Tiberias** is not even the greatest surprise the day holds for you. You continue driving, now up steep mountain roads, until you come to the town of **Meron**. There, your son-in-law leads his son to an open-air barber, who cuts off the hair that has been growing on his head since his birth. "It is a custom," you learn, "to come here on **Lag BaOmer** and give little boys their first haircuts. The hair is burned, and the child is ready to learn his *alef-bet*."

If something even more unusual happens to your family, turn to page 147.

If, on the other hand, the distance between you and your daughter's family grows greater, turn to page 116.

91

The Jews who live in this area of **Tel Aviv** are poor. Most of the older ones have immigrated from Arab lands, especially **Morocco**, and the promise of Israel has not yet filtered down to them. Many children run through the crowded markets, while their parents despair that their youngsters will ever find a better life. Many of these **Sephardic** Jews turn for their only hope to **Orthodox** Judaism mixed with superstitions that they had brought from their former homelands.

A new political party formed by **Sephardic** Jews, known as Shas, has begun to work among these people. Of course, its leaders want their votes. But they have determined that the best way to gain the support of these citizens is to help them with the necessities of life. Shas opens service centers in various neighborhoods, little offices where the residents can come to get help with food and clothing and housing, with schools for their children and health care for themselves and their parents. For the first time, the people feel, someone has their interests at heart, someone really cares about them.

Shas leaders are soon elected to the **Knesset**, and the people watch with pride as these officials exercise enough power to gain financial grants for the neighborhood. Your son-in-law is deeply involved, helping on many fronts. Shas not only contributes to the welfare of the people, but also gives him a great sense of achievement, of having done a real **mitzvah**. He even plans a political career for himself.

If his work with Shas leads him to power, but also has an unfortunate outcome, turn to page 131.

If he is able to remain untouched by the rumors about misuse of money that soon surface, turn to page 138.

92

Like many Jews in your community, you contribute to the annual campaign of the Jewish **Federation**. Much of the money they raise stays in your city to support Jewish services—the home for the aged, the Jewish community center, Jewish education, etc.—but a good part of it also goes to help Jews in Israel and elsewhere. Making sure that the human needs of your fellow Jews are met is an important aspect of *tzedakah,* and you actively try to convince others to help generously.

One day, you receive a telephone call from the director of the **Federation**. He invites you to his office, and there, he tells you he has an idea. "I've been impressed with your dedication to our efforts and your ability to persuade others. We need someone to work with us to counsel young Jews who are going to visit Israel. Most of them will simply go for a visit and then come back; others will stay for six months or a year to study or volunteer; some may decide to make *aliyah.* I think you could be very important to them by giving them advice before they go and then helping them use their experiences when they return. What do you think?"

It's the opportunity you've been looking for. You can stay in America with your family and you can help Israel at the same time. It sounds perfect. Most of what you do in this new job gives you great pleasure, but one thing worries you: very few young American Jews are willing to move to Israel permanently. *Aliyah* is a key part of **Zionism**, but it doesn't seem to be happening.

*If you choose to remain in the **United States** for the rest of your life, turn to page 172.*

If you wait only until a new opportunity to help Israel is offered to you, turn to page 173.

93

Like all Israelis who have finished their active military service, you are obligated to remain in the reserve *(miluim)* until you are 50. One month each year, you are required to put on your uniform and become an active soldier again. You never know where you will be sent or what your duty will be, but you are proud to do your part to help protect Israel.

As time goes on and you get a little older, active military life becomes harder. You are not quite as agile as you were before, nor do you have the physical endurance to handle the tasks. But you are not willing to admit that your age is taking its toll, so you engage in a program of daily exercise, and one day a week you play soccer with some friends. As you enter your forties, you look in the mirror and admire the muscles in your body; you have entered middle-age rather gracefully.

The commanders of your military unit seem to think so too. During your *miluim* duty, they assign you to train a younger commando group. You take them on long hikes through the hills of the **Galilee**, teaching them how to spot terrorists trying to sneak into the country. Over the years, you've learned a few tricks about resisting infiltrators who would plant bombs and do other damage in Israeli towns and villages; now it is your chance to share this knowledge with the next generation, and you gladly do so. You believe you know how Arab people think, and you want the younger soldiers to have the benefit of your wisdom.

If you also choose to share your perspective with your daughter as you watch something special on the television, turn to page 13.

If this knowledge causes you to be placed in a dangerous situation, turn to page 22.

94

Like all Israelis, you have continued your military service in the Army reserve, the *miluim*. Now, as raids from the north become more frequent, you are called back to active army service and sent to a base not very far south of the border with **Lebanon**. The task your unit is assigned is to prevent squads of Arab guerillas from crossing the border, entering settlements and causing damage. Already, a number of Israelis have been killed and wounded in such attacks, and a great deal of agricultural machinery on the **kibbutzim** has been destroyed.

To help you achieve your goal, you recruit a number of trackers from nearby Druze villages of the northern **Galilee**. The Druze are Arabs, but they have their own, different religious practices. They are Israeli citizens who are loyal to the new country. They know every centimeter of the land, and they are tireless and very skilled as scouts. Without them, your task would be a great deal more difficult.

> *As you work with these Druze scouts, you realize how foreign you are to this region of the world. In many ways, you are still a European; you have not had the chance really to become at home in the Middle East. To gain some new skills that will help you in this regard, turn to page 61.*

> *If this military work with Arab Israelis teaches you that different people can live in peace and that helping this to happen should be the goal of your life, turn to page 69.*

95

The Arabs who have remained in the new State of Israel confuse you. When you visit them in their houses, they offer hospitality, conversation, and apparent friendship. As you sit together, dipping food from the common, central bowl in the middle of the table, surrounded by smiling children and silent women, you become more and more aware of the human qualities that all people have in common. "These should not be enemies," you think to yourself. "We share so many things that we ought to be friends."

But, when you leave their homes and walk the streets of their neighborhoods, you sense angry stares and even wonder about your safety. Are you imagining that a darker side of these Arabs lurks only barely concealed beneath the surface? Perhaps both friendship and mistrust exist together among this community, which sees you as a human being, but also as an intruder who has taken what they believe to be their land.

Occasional acts of violence break out, particularly in areas where there are lots of young men who cannot imagine a bright future for themselves. Some of them have left school in their early teens; they will likely never have a good job. The only thing that will make them feel good about themselves is resisting the Israelis.

If you worry so much about these groups of young men that you want to devote your efforts to protecting Israel against them, turn to page 70.

If you think that they must be getting help from outside the country and you seek to cut off those supplies, turn to page 169.

96

One Wednesday afternoon, all of you drive up to **Jerusalem** in the **kibbutz**'s van. On Thursday morning, the Torah is read at **Reform** congregation **Har El** as your son and future daughter-in-law sit together during services. Then, you all walk to the offices of the **Rabbanut**, where you suffer through two hours of filling out papers and answering questions—the same questions over and over again. *Savlanut,* patience.

An **Orthodox** rabbi no one of you has ever seen before appears and lines everyone up under a *chuppah*. In Hebrew that is so fast you can hardly distinguish one word from the next, he recites the seven wedding blessings and declares that the couple is married.

"We may be husband and wife in the eyes of the State of Israel," your son protests as soon as you are outside the building, "but it doesn't seem right. There was nothing in that ceremony that seemed holy; I wonder if God was even present. Let's go back to our own home and our own rabbi and figure out how to do this right."

And so, Friday morning, all the residents of **Yahel** gather at the synagogue of the **kibbutz**, while the rabbi and the young couple come together lovingly under a *chuppah* made by friends from the **kibbutz**. "This is different," you say to your wife. "This feels like family, and it feels like God is among us."

You and your family and the rest of the **kibbutzniks** rejoice with the bride and groom and vow to spend the rest of your lives creating a Jewish state in which liberal Judaism will have a vital and respected role.

END

Jewish law, the **halachah**, is pretty clear. It is required that the sacred quality of the human being, whether alive or dead, be respected. Cutting up a dead body is prohibited. After all, the body is made "in the image of God," and any disrespect shown toward the body is, in the end, disrespect toward God.

Yet there is another principle of the **halachah**. The highest value of Judaism is *pikuach nefesh*, "saving a life." One is even permitted to dig with a shovel on **Yom Kippur** if one suspects that a person might be buried in the rubble of an earthquake. Certainly, in this case where two lives would be saved, the idea of *pikuach nefesh* should be given a higher value than even the holiness of the human body.

The rabbinical council, an assembly of some of the most respected **Orthodox** rabbis in Israel, gathers quickly in the conference room of the **Rabbanut**. These men are in their sixties and seventies, and they have spent their entire adult lives trying to apply Jewish legal ideas to real-life situations. They stroke their beards and sway back and forth gently as they listen to each other's arguments. They know that they must choose one of these high principles of Judaism over another; it is a very critical matter they are called upon to consider, and they take their responsibility seriously.

Just as they are about to reach a decision, a doctor who has been helping them understand technical, medical issues raises a point that makes their decision even more difficult.

To follow the problem he describes, turn to page 119.

98

The mayor of **Jerusalem** has a tradition of opening his home on **Shabbat** afternoon to anyone who wants to come in for conversation and a cup of tea. You take advantage of this opening. There are usually interesting people at **Teddy Kollek**'s house, and this particular afternoon is no different. One man especially intrigues you. He is about six feet tall with amazing eyebrows. When he speaks, they seem to move with each word, arching up and down in rhythm.

You introduce yourself to **Dr. Nelson Glueck**, who turns out to be a world-famous archaeologist. After he gets to know you, he invites to you come down to the dig he is working on at **Tel Gezer**, an ancient fortress city to the east of **Tel Aviv**. As you work with him there, he explains to you what he believes. "The more I find out from my scientific explorations, the more I come to trust the history that is told in the Bible. If we read Scripture carefully, we can find out a great deal about Israel's ancient past. In fact, if we learn about the history of our people, we shall be able to see how Judaism developed and grew from its biblical roots to the religion it is today."

You had never thought of Judaism as a changing, growing process. But now that you think of it, why should religion be unchanging when everything else in life moves and grows? **Glueck** explains to you that this idea is the basis for **Reform Judaism**.

*To follow **Glueck**'s vision, turn to page 148.*

Or, you can walk another path into the past of your people by turning to page 25.

99

Because you are a trained and experienced pilot, you are able to travel back to Israel with no delay. They do need you, and soon you find yourself flying a jet plane over the **Golan**, hunting Syrian tanks with your Sidewinder missiles. You use the plane's electronic aiming system skillfully; within a few days, you are one of the most successful pilots in this air-to-ground combat.

Within six days, the combined Arab armies call for a truce. They had tried to surprise Israel, but the real surprise was on them. Israel was able to take control of the battlefields and defeat its enemies. In fact, Israel's victory is so vast that new territories fall under its control. It is nice to have the **West Bank** of the **Jordan River**, the **Sinai**, and the **Golan**; Israel will be safer with these additional regions on its borders. But the **Old City of Jerusalem** is the real prize, and nothing will be more exciting than visiting *Hakotel*, the Temple's **Western Wall**.

Jerusalem is special, but you cannot shake the vision of the area just west of the **Golan**'s capital town, **Kuneitra**. You decide to settle there with your family in one of the newly developed towns and plant a vineyard. You remember the **prophet Jeremiah**, who always looked to the future. Grape vines will take a while to grow and produce fruit. Planting them in Israel's holy soil and tending them carefully is your way of providing for your children and grandchildren, of making sure that they will always live in this wonderful land and care for it. Planting roots in the Land of Israel makes you very happy, and you live out the rest of your life, producing wine and loving your family.

END

100

W hen you arrive at **Lod Airport** in **Lod**, near **Tel Aviv**, one of your friends from the air force takes you aside. "I've got to show you this new airplane that I am learning to fly." You climb into the cockpit with him and gasp as you look at the controls. Almost everything is controlled by a computer. It's not the kind of airplane you had learned to fly. But this must be the wave of the future.

Fortunately, Israel's armed forces win a nearly miraculous victory in only six days. The entire country celebrates, and so do you. Not only has Israel won an incredible victory, but you have also found something to which you want to dedicate your life. Computers will be the world of tomorrow, you conclude, and you want to be involved with them.

Your family decides to join you in Israel. You secure a job with a company in **Ramat Gan** and spend almost all your spare time reading about these marvelous electronic devices. Israel may be a small country, you think, but with these tiny computers, we shall be able to defend ourselves. You spend the rest of your life working with computers and teaching your children and grandchildren how to use them. It feels very special that your work has helped Israel protect itself and that your next generations are experts in how to use these marvels. Your life has moved from **Poland** to **Germany** to Palestine to **America** and back to Israel. Each step has been a wonderful adventure, and you thank God that you have been able to live such a full and meaningful life.

END

101

There are still tens of thousands of Jews in Europe, survivors of the *Shoah,* who need to find permanent new homelands. Many of them, you believe, ought to follow your path and make *aliyah* to Israel. But how to help them accomplish that goal?

One day, as you are talking with a group of workers in **Petach Tikva,** you accidentally learn that Israel will be sending a diplomatic mission to **Geneva** to assist these refugees. You immediately return to **Jerusalem** and secure a job with the delegation as a translator. Its leader is a brilliant young diplomat named **Abba Eban,** himself an immigrant from **South Africa.** He explains that all of you will be working with two other organizations, the **United Nations International Refugee Organization** and the Jewish **Joint Distribution Committee.** Together you will close the last of the **displaced persons' camps,** reunite the survivors with any family you can find anywhere in the world, and bring those who are alone to Israel. There, at least, they will be among other Jews; there they will have a substitute family to care for them.

The work you do with these Jewish refugees is tremendously satisfying—so much so that you decide to devote the rest of your life to this kind of effort.

If you join another Israeli rescue team, turn to page 153.

If you elect to share Israel's experience with refugee resettlement with other nations, turn to page 154.

102

Mrs. Meir summons you to her office. "I know you have been working very hard to organize the workers and protect their welfare. But I have a new challenge for you. I have been selected to be the first Israeli diplomatic representative in **Moscow**. I shall need a staff to help me, and I want you to come with me. Your ability with the Russian and Polish languages will be a great help."

You are overjoyed at this important assignment. It is late September when all of you arrive in the Russian capital. At the Foreign Ministry, you are greeted cordially by the Russian officials, but it is at the synagogue and the Jewish theater where the reception is overwhelming. Crowds of Jews cheer loudly for **Mrs. Meir** and for the State of Israel.

Russian authorities are not pleased by this display of intense affection and support. They close down a **Yiddish** newspaper and arrest the leaders of the **Jewish Anti-Fascist Committee**. It's their way of sending a very clear message: too much interest in Israel could be dangerous to Russian Jews.

As much as the Russian government wants good relations with the new country of Israel, they are also concerned about what the Arab countries will think; **Russia** wants friendship with those nations, too. And then there is the age-old problem of Russian anti-Semitism; a history of **pogroms** and discrimination reminds you that **Russia** has not been a safe place for Jews to live.

If you try to establish connections to the leaders of Russian Jewry, turn to page 105.

If you try to behave very properly, but something bad happens anyway, turn to page 28.

103

A committee of business executives comes to visit you. They represent the Zim Line, the company that is planning to build an ocean liner for Israel. The plan is that tourists from America will travel to Israel on an Israeli ship and that the ship will also take cruises throughout the **Mediterranean**. They propose that you be in charge of all the art and decoration of this new vessel.

"But where," you ask, "will the money for this project come from?" "Don't worry," a short, bald man answers. Clearly, he is an American. You soon understand that **Gottlieb Hammer** has connections with American bankers and that he will raise the money for this project, as he has for many other activities, even for the purchase of guns during the **War of Independence**.

The work goes slowly. There are committees that must pass on every idea. They love to argue, and that takes time. While you are waiting for them to decide, you drink a lemonade in the warm summer breeze of an outdoor café. A young woman walks up to you and asks: "May I sit at your table?" You stand up, greet her, and offer her a seat. Soon, you are deep in conversation, for she is very attractive. Before long, you are seeing each other almost every day, and you are aware that your smile is broader and that there is a bounce in your step. Even your art work seems happier.

Neither of you has any doubt as you stand under the *chuppah*. Your life is fulfilled. But eighteen months later, life gets even better when your daughter is born.

If you want to settle down and stop working on the Shalom, *turn to page 67.*

If you feel you must complete the Shalom *project, turn to page 183.*

104

When the young couple returns to **Haifa**, they remember the awful conditions of black African life. "If only these people had a way to grow their own food, their lives would be so much easier. There is something we can do to help. After all, our **kibbutzim** have learned how to produce crops from rocky soil. We could share our knowledge with the people of the townships."

With the help of the minister of agriculture, your daughter and her friends are able to organize teams of Israeli scientists and farmers. The government sends them to **Soweto** and to other similar places so that they can teach other people the lessons they have learned. "If we can give people hope for a better life, perhaps they will not feel the need for a violent and bloody revolution. And perhaps they will not attack the Jewish community when change comes—and it will come."

The revolution in **South Africa** is remarkably peaceful. To everyone's surprise, the white leadership transfers power to black leaders without a fight. You wonder if the agricultural projects made a difference. There's no way to know, but you are grateful that your children worked to fulfill **Moses Maimonides**' highest level of *tzedakah*, to help a needy person avoid taking charity by teaching that person how to support himself or herself. You have raised children who understand that basic Jewish idea, and that makes you enormously satisfied with your own life.

END

105

You know that the Russian secret police are watching the synagogue, noting who is there, who sits next to each other, what foreign Jews come to services. That's the last place you ought to talk to the leaders of the community. Instead, you walk through muddy streets, double back on yourself, and stop several times; it doesn't seem that anyone is following you. Finally, you climb the stairs to a small apartment off the Arbat; the crowds of pedestrians have made it possible for you to escape the secret police who were tailing you.

The **Communist Party** teaches that religion is a useless and bad activity, that it is only helpful to control the masses of people. Intelligent and modern people, they say, should not need religion. But the Jews of **Moscow** don't seem to have learned this message. They want to speak Hebrew, pray the traditional verses, hear Jewish music, and go to Jewish plays.

To do these things, however, is dangerous. At any time, the police could swoop down on them, arrest them for anti-Soviet activities, and send them to prison in **Siberia**. Still, the Jews of **Russia** will not give up their heritage. Secretly, you supply them with materials to study. They want to remain Jewish; Israel and the rest of the world's Jews want to help them to be Jews. But it is not easy.

*After **Josef Stalin** dies in 1953, the danger increases. If you try to help Russian Jews escape, turn to page 106.*

*If you want to help the many Jews who cannot or will not leave **Russia**, turn to page 143.*

106

For thirty years, you work in the Israeli embassy in **Moscow**. Your official title is "Cultural Officer," but your real work is to help any Jew who wants to leave. It is very difficult for Jews to emigrate, but you arrange for documents (so what if they are false!) that tell of relatives in other lands. Each person you help will depart for a family reunion. Large sums of money must be paid for the right permits. These are, in fact, bribes, but anything is permitted to get a Jew out of captivity. Engaging in *pidyon sh'vuyim*, "the ransom of prisoners," is an age-old **mitzvah**.

One by one, two by two, they leave, and with each departure you feel that you have saved lives. But there are millions more who hope for the same escape. Occasionally, to gain some favor with the **United States** or other countries, **Russia** allows a few thousand Jews to leave, mostly through **Vienna, Austria**. But the doors close just as quickly as they open.

Then, suddenly, in 1989, the Union of Soviet Socialist Republics falls apart. Michael Gorbachev, the new premier of **Russia**, permits open emigration, and hundreds of Jews crowd onto airplanes and trains every day. You have lived long enough to see the fulfillment of your dreams.

Now, there is a new challenge—helping the Russian Jews who have immigrated to Israel settle into their new lives.

To see what role you have in this process, turn to page 178.

107

Though your daughter lives with you at **Neve Shalom/Wahat al-Salaam**, she's like teenagers all over the world. She spends hours reading movie magazines and talking with her friends about the most recent activities of the stars. As she gets a little older, she grows beyond these youthful crushes, but you can tell that she's still in love with being in love.

A young man from the **Netherlands** comes to spend a few weeks at the **kibbutz**, and your daughter falls madly in love with him. You imagine that this is a passing phase, but, in fact, she continues to correspond with him and their relationship becomes serious. He's not exactly your idea of the man your daughter should marry—not a **kibbutznik**, not an Israeli, from a distant land—but they love each other. It could be worse.

When they marry, they surprise you. "We're so in love that we're going to go into the business of love. We're going to represent a Dutch-Jewish diamond merchant by opening an office in a suburb of **Haifa**. What a wonderful feeling it will be to know that lovers all over the world will be wearing rings with our stones in them."

Their business branches out. Not only do they have connections with jewelers in **Antwerp** and **Amsterdam**, but soon they start doing a lot of business with companies in **South Africa**. Their work occasionally takes them to these locations to meet with their partners. While you are always worried about their safety on such long overseas trips, you are happy that they will be with fellow Jews at their destinations; you know that they will be well taken care of.

If something changes their lives during a trip to **South Africa**, *turn to page 18.*

On their first visit to **Amsterdam**, *they have a new experience. To find out what it is, turn to page 121.*

108

On the **Golan Heights**, there are new Israeli settlers, many of them living in **kibbutzim**, and Arabs whose families have lived there for hundreds of years. As you and your team of trained interns drive from village to village, you are almost run off the narrow road by a tanker truck. "What was that?" you ask. "That was a water truck," one of them answers. "There are no natural rivers or streams in this area, so all the water has to be brought in by truck."

Aha! There's a great idea for a joint community development project. With help from the faculty of the **Technion** in **Haifa**, you discover three sites where there is, in fact, water under the rocky soil. "We can dig wells at these places and supply water to the villages and vineyards that are nearby. With water, they can grow and develop; perhaps they can even start new businesses."

Your interns visit both Israeli and Arab settlements and talk about the project. Lots of people are surprised that Arabs and Israelis are willing to work together to dig the wells, but you are not. "Why should they share the effort? Because they will both share the rewards!"

The wells are dug and water gushes out, into pipelines, into both Arab and Israeli villages, into homes and offices. You are realistic. Digging a few wells has not quenched decades of fiery feelings between these two groups, but maybe it has started to erode the hatred that has built up over the years. After all, the Bible called these *mayim chayim,* "life-giving waters," and what is more precious to life than peace? You and your team are convinced that you have done something important, that you have helped these villagers take a few steps down the road toward *shalom.*

END

109

When you return to the farm, you survey the property. On the west side, there is a big barn where you have been storing bags of barley before they are taken away to market. You could easily convert this barn into a factory. All it would take is some money!

You go to the library and borrow a few books about managing a company. The first thing they tell you to do is to create a business plan, so you spend some time thinking about how this new factory will work, where its materials will come from, who will do the work, how you will sell the products, what money it will require, and how much profit can be expected. You take this plan back to **Tel Aviv** and meet with a man who is called a venture capitalist. He finds money to invest in new businesses, and he likes your idea. It turns out that his son smashed up his own car just last week, and he has been having trouble finding parts to make the repairs. Your timing is superb!

Soon you are turning out parts for the grill and headlights of small, imported cars. After all, you reasoned in your business plan, most of the crashes involve the front end of vehicles, so parts for the front are probably most in demand. You were right. The factory is very successful.

As money flows into the **kibbutz**, something unexpected happens. The lifestyle of the members of the communal settlement changes. They want color televisions and vacations. They even want to hire workers so they no longer have to do the hard work themselves. Slowly, the character of the **kibbutz** shifts.

To follow this change, turn to page 72.

110

The Supreme Court rules that Brother Daniel is no longer a Jew. He made that decision himself, they declare, when he remained a Catholic after the war. When he could have returned to Judaism, he did not, and that is what counts.

But he is still a hero. And there is a place in Israel where the heroes of World War II are recognized. That place is called **Yad Vashem**, and each non-Jewish hero has a tree with a plaque at its base. Those who are still alive have come to witness the planting of their trees and to receive a medal and a certificate. They are called "righteous gentiles."

You and other Polish survivors who know firsthand of Brother Daniel's courageous actions write letters to **Yad Vashem**. If anyone deserves a tree, this man does, and you are determined to see that he receives that honor.

But an unexpected problem arises. When Brother Daniel performed his heroic acts in **Warsaw**, he was still Oswald the Jew. He only became a gentile later. So, how can he receive an honor that is meant for a gentile when he was a Jew? What a dilemma!

After much discussion, the board of directors of **Yad Vashem** comes up with a decision so wise that it is worthy of King Solomon. "We cannot honor him as a righteous gentile, because he wasn't. But we must honor him. So, we shall create a special space for him and him alone. He shall have a tree there and a special plaque."

Finally, on a very proud Sunday afternoon, you gather at **Yad Vashem** to honor Brother Daniel in this way. Tears flow as you grasp each other. "I am so glad this has happened," you tell him. "In a way, I feel that I have at last repaid a long-standing debt."

END

111

Y our daughter and her husband come back to Israel and share their fears with you. "We think there is going to be a real problem for the Jews of **South Africa**. There are over a hundred thousand Jews there, and they are in great peril. We must help them get ready to flee their country if something really bad happens."

The Jews of **South Africa** are very strong supporters of **Zionism**. They come to Israel frequently, and some of them even own apartments in **Jerusalem** and **Tel Aviv**. This gives your daughter an idea. "These Jews will gladly invest in the building of the Jewish state. If we can arrange for them to purchase a large sum of State of Israel Bonds, their money would come here to build schools and hospitals and roads. As **Zionists**, the Jews of **South Africa** would certainly like to support the Jewish state in this way. But, if they do have to leave quickly, they will have money invested here that will help them start their new lives. It's a winning arrangement for everyone!"

The transition from white rule to a black government in **South Africa** occurs relatively easily and peacefully. The worst fears about the safety of the Jewish community do not come to pass, but you are immensely proud of your daughter and her friends. They have fulfilled one of the most important **mitzvot**, that of *pikuach nefesh*, "helping to save a life." With young people like these in Israel, the Jewish quality of this state is assured for a long time in the future.

END

112

Agents of the British intelligence services actively patrol all the ports in **Italy**, hoping to identify ships that will leave carrying illegal immigrants to Palestine. They pass this information on to the British navy ships that blockade the coastline of Palestine, and nearly all the ships are intercepted.

You and the other passengers on the *Exodus* realize that the chances of getting into Palestine are slim, but there is another goal you have in mind. "If we are caught, we must make sure that our fate is published in every newspaper in the world. Photographs of desperate concentration camp survivors will rally support for the **Zionist** cause." And, true to your plans, when your ship is seized by a British patrol boat and towed into **Haifa** harbor, it is festooned with signs: "Death is no stranger to us. Nothing can keep us from our Jewish homeland. The blood be on your head if you fire on this unarmed ship."

No one is allowed to leave the ship. British soldiers are stationed on the dock every six feet, and you understand that anyone trying to escape will be shot. Soon, the ship leaves the dock, sails back out to sea and puts in on the island of **Cyprus**. You are marched to a camp that is scarcely better than the concentration camps you knew in **Nazi Germany**, but at least they give you food and medical care.

One group of Jewish prisoners meets every night to plot an escape. If you join them, turn to page 118.

If, on the other hand, you think you have cheated death enough times and that it would be safer just to wait for the end of this imprisonment, turn to page 149.

113

"We've had enough of this dry desert," some of the scientists complain to you. "We need a break. Let's drive down to **Eilat**, where we can sit on the beach and swim in the sea." Why not! Maybe a change of scenery would help them think of solutions. After all, the Rabbis taught, "If you change your place, you might change your luck."

One of the scientists plunges into the **Gulf of Aqaba** and ducks under the surface. He comes up sputtering and spitting out water, but smiling. "Are you crazy?" his friends ask. "Maybe," he says, "but I think I may have found our solution. Do you remember when we all went swimming in the **Dead Sea**? It was so salty that we were warned not to put our heads under the water. Here, however, I could do that. This water is salty, but not nearly as much as there. Something has happened to take a lot of the salt out of this water. If we could only figure out how to remove the rest of the chemicals, we'd have all the fresh water we could ever use."

They grab a pencil and a couple of paper napkins at the beach restaurant and start working on equations and graphs and numbers and all sorts of ideas. The problem is that they know how to get the salt out of the water, but the solutions all cost too much. "We'll keep at it," they say. "Soon, we'll come up with an answer that will work and be cheap enough to be reasonable. Don't give up hope. We're going to make this possible."

And so you spend the rest of your life working with this team of scientists as they work to solve Israel's water problems and make the desert come alive with flowers and crops.

END

114

There are two ways to create electricity other than burning fossil fuels like oil and gas: the wind and the sun. And there is plenty of each here at **Yahel**. In fact, when it is really hot outside, you wish sometimes that there would be just a little less sun! Whew! The temperature can be well over a hundred degrees for day after day.

The group of scientists with whom you are working cannot decide which source of alternative power might be the best. Some of them are in favor of building an entire forest of windmills, giant turbines as tall as a fifteen-story building, with propellers on top that will turn all the time. "We could erect hundreds of these machines, and we would have an inexhaustible source of energy."

"But, my friend," one of the others objects. "The turbines will break. With solar collector panels, there are no moving parts. Once we build them and set them out on the desert floor, there will be nothing more to do—just wait for the electricity to flow through the wires, into the pumps. And then the desert will be covered with vegetables and flowers and all sorts of growing things. It couldn't be easier."

Well, scientists being scientists, they don't agree. You can see the good and bad points of each solution, and you decide that you will dedicate the rest of your life to testing both ideas. Maybe there will be clear evidence that one works better than the other. In any event, the future of the region, maybe the entire nation, will depend on your success.

END

115

One of the men who sits across the coffee table from you during these debates is a slight, balding man named **Menachem Begin**. For a long time, he refuses to tell you what he does during the day. Eventually, however, he comes to trust you, and he reveals that he is the head of a secret military organization called **Irgun Tz'va-i L'umi**. He believes that the leaders of the *yishuv*, people like **David Ben-Gurion**, cooperate too easily with the British. "The only way we shall drive the British out of Palestine," **Begin** informs you with steely determination, "is by force. If the price they have to pay to stay here is too high, then they will pull out. We shall exact that price from them."

You come to the conclusion that **Begin** is right. "The German enemy murdered my family; now, another enemy wants to kill more of my people, and the British are protecting them. I will not, I cannot let that happen. Never again will we fail to resist tyrants in the most active and strongest way!"

Inspired by **Begin**, you join the **Irgun** to fight for your new homeland. In a series of daring raids, you and the other **Irgun** members dynamite a series of small British forts. Some of their soldiers are killed and more are wounded, but you conclude that this is the necessary cost of forcing an end to the British **Mandate**. Whether your actions were decisive or not, the British withdraw, and the State of Israel is born on May 14, 1948.

You may decide to remain in the new Israeli army after independence. If you do, turn to page 157.

On the other hand, if you think there is a better way to protect the new country, turn to page 159.

116

Your son-in-law falls in love with the teachings of a Jewish holy man who lived in **Morocco**. Whatever he thinks this dead saint might want him to do, he obeys. This deeply worries you. Over dinner one night, you speak your mind. "This reminds me of what happened in **Germany** before World War II. The people did whatever **Adolf Hitler** told them to do without questioning a thing. Even when the orders were evil, they did what they were told. It was blind obedience—and it turned out to be a terrible disaster for our people. I know. I was there."

When he hears your remarks, your son-in-law is upset. "I have a right to my beliefs. You have no right to try to change them." He pushes his chair back from the table and leaves the room. Your daughter follows him. She tries to calm him down, but he is very angry. It is possible that you have said the wrong thing, that this has caused a serious split in the family.

But it is also possible that he will think about what you have said in the days to come and will see that you have a point. Will your comments change his way of thinking? Will they alter his behavior? Maybe . . . maybe not. To have said what you did may be all that you can do in this situation. But that is also the least you can do. You have had the courage of your convictions and been honest with a person you really do care about. You are at peace with yourself because you have done the right thing.

END

117

The **War of Independence** is over, but you will never be free of its memories. You have seen the horrors of war, the death and destruction, the maiming wounds inflicted on young people, the scars of loss left on an entire country. You know, of course, that this war was not of Israel's doing. The Arab armies attacked, and Israel had to defend itself. But you think that there must be a better way.

With the help of friends you made in the army, you secure a low-level appointment to a very important diplomatic team. Quietly, without publicity, this group will travel to **Amman**, capital of **Jordan**, to meet with **King Abdullah**. This ruler seems to have a broader vision; he is willing to talk with Israel about peace.

Before your team can leave **Jerusalem**, however, a sad report comes over the news. Arab radicals have assassinated the king. The trip to **Amman** will not occur, at least not for many, many years.

The death of **Abdullah** only strengthens your conviction that war is not the way. You are more committed than ever to the pursuit of peace. Something you learned in *cheder*, years before, comes to your mind. "Be among the disciples of Aaron," the rabbis said. "Always pursue the path of peace." The way of *shalom*, you are absolutely sure, is the only way your grandchildren will be spared the terrible horrors of war.

If you think that you can best express your longing for peace through art, turn to page 83.

On the other hand, if you cannot pursue peace with others until you have found peace within yourself and with your own experiences, turn to page 85.

118

Some of the British guards are really very decent chaps. They don't agree with the policy of their government and secretly tell you that they are on your side. You know that any escape plan must count on these guards looking the other way, at just the right time.

Word is passed to your group that a small boat will be waiting in the port of a village near the internment camp. If you can make it to the boat, those on board will try to sneak you into Palestine. It's worth a try. While the friendly British guards happen to be busy somewhere else, twenty of you crawl under the fence and slip down the hill to the port. There, indeed, a small fishing boat is waiting. On deck is a young **Haganah** officer named **Yitzchak Rabin**. You already know him as a daring, courageous leader; his reputation has led the British army in Palestine to offer a reward for his arrest.

Without a sound and with no lights, your boat approaches the coastline of Palestine. Not a British ship is in sight; you are very lucky that you have made it this far undetected. About a hundred meters from the shore, **Rabin** orders everyone to jump into the water. "The only way is to swim. Good luck, boys! Our people will meet you on the shore." And swim you do, until it feels like your arms will fall off. When you put your feet down, you feel the sandy bottom and you stride out of the water, onto the land of the Jewish people and into the arms of friendly **Haganah** forces.

*One possibility is to hide in the **Old City of Jerusalem**. Among the many people there, you can probably disappear effectively. If that is your choice, turn to page 75.*

*Another option is to go to an isolated **kibbutz**. The British are unlikely to find you there. If you choose that route, turn to page 124.*

119

"We have identified two people who are our primary candidates for the transplant of these kidneys. One is an Israeli man. No problem. But the second person is a young Palestinian woman. She is the daughter of one of the Arab leaders of **Hebron**. No one thinks that her father actually fired the shot that killed Yaron, but all of us realize that he was involved. He gave fiery talks to the young Palestinians; he urged them to resist the Israeli settlers in any way possible. Can we have any doubt that his words incited one of the young militants to pull the trigger? Can we give a kidney from this young Israeli to the daughter of the man who, at least indirectly, was responsible for his murder?"

What a dilemma! The Palestinian girl desperately needs the kidney. Without it, she will probably die. But should she benefit from a bodily organ of someone who died because of her own father's hate-filled words? Might it not be a better idea to find a second recipient whose need is just about as great, but whose family was not involved in this shooting?

If you press your ear to the door, hoping to hear the decision of the rabbis, turn to page 7.

If you walk away, amazed that they would even consider giving the kidney to such a person, turn to page 120.

120

As you walk away from the conference room, you are aware of a group of **Chasidic** Jews walking alongside you. "Can you believe that the rabbis are even considering this request?" one man shouts. He is so angry that his black hat perches dangerously to the side, knocked off center by the vigorous shaking of his head. "If they approve this transplant, it will be a *chilul HaShem,* an insult to God. And what's more, who is to know what further cases will be brought to them? If they open the door now, there will be more requests, and more abuses, and more bad decisions. We may lose this case, but we will never agree that it is the right way to go. The **halachah** leads down a different path; that is the only direction in which the Holy and Blessed One of Israel permits us to go."

In fact, the decision flies in the face of their opposition, but they vow to continue to stand firm. You admire their commitment. They know what they believe, and they will not move. Right is right, and wrong is wrong; and for these Jews, there is no middle ground, no compromise.

The decision of the rabbinical court of Jerusalem has provoked a great controversy. People heatedly debate whether the court was right or wrong. You just laugh. "Jewish life has always been this way," you say. "No matter when or where, we have always found something to argue about. When people care passionately about their faith, that is what happens. It will be an awful day when Jews don't care enough to fight with each other!"

END

121

The first stop the young couple make in **Amsterdam** is the house where **Anne Frank** and her family hid during most of World War II. "My father went through something like this himself," your daughter says. "I have to see for myself what it must have been like. It's part of my family's story. It's almost like a religious pilgrimage for me."

As they stand outside, leaning on the railing next to the canal, a man old enough to be her father engages them in conversation. "I come here often," he says. "It reminds me of the courage of many people I knew during the *Shoah.*" When he uses this Hebrew word, they realize he is Jewish, and your son-in-law remarks that you, too, had been in the camps. In what can only be called a "small-world story," it turns out that he knew you in **Belsen** and later in Zeilsheim; you were actually friends a generation ago.

He has also begun a new life, here in the **Netherlands**, and he now has children your daughter's age. "You must come to my house for **Shabbat** dinner," he tells your daughter and son-in-law. "You cannot eat in a restaurant on Friday night!" And so they rekindle, in a new place and in a new time, the relationship that you had so many years ago under much less pleasant circumstances.

It turns out that this man, like many Jews in **Holland**, is a diamond broker. He engages your daughter and son-in-law to use their office in **Haifa** for his business.

If you find an interesting surprise in this new activity, turn to page 145.

On the other hand, if romance in the diamond business continues, turn to page 146.

W hen she arrives at school, your daughter and her classmates board a bus. "Don't worry," the teacher says. "The trip will not be long—at least in terms of distance. But we shall be going almost three thousand years back in time."

The bus winds its way up a narrow dusty road toward the top of a large hill. "This place was one of **King Solomon**'s fortress cities," explains the guide. "It is called **Megiddo**. Along with the two other cities of **Hazor** and **Gezer**, Israel's most powerful king could control all the traffic between **Egypt** and **Mesopotamia**. In its time, this was a really important place. We are only now beginning to excavate the *tel*, but we expect to find amazing things."

Your daughter is a curious young woman. She strays from the group and pokes about in the corner of a pile of stones. A strange shape juts out, and she calls to the guide. "Come look! What do you suppose this is?" The guide needs only a quick look to realize that this might be a valuable find. She immediately summons the scholars who are in charge of the dig, and they unearth the find very carefully, lifting the rocks and brushing away the dirt. "**Ashtarte**," one of them cries out, "a goddess of fertility. It proves that this area was farmed in biblical times, just as it is now. Farmers believed that this statuette would help their crops succeed."

Your daughter tells you about this find. She is really excited. "*Abba*, I'm going to go to the **Hebrew University** and study archaeology. This is all part of our national history, and it is part of what makes our new country great today."

If she graduates and wants to excavate in Jerusalem, turn to page 76.

If she falls in love and puts her career on hold for a while, turn to page 36.

123

Agriculture is no longer as profitable as it once was. It used to be that idealistic young Israelis would come to work on the farm just for the satisfaction of building up the new country and turning the landscape green. Now you have to pay Arab workers from the nearby villages to do the same tasks. The cost of labor rises every year. If there is not enough rain to grow your crops—and there usually isn't—you have to buy water for irrigation. It's expensive. This is a time when you need to be creative if you are to continue living here.

On a trip to **Tel Aviv** to visit your cousin, you watch as young men and women walk up and down the streets, talking on their mobile telephones and answering their pagers. A parade of fancy cars drives past, and you watch them with envy. You certainly cannot afford to buy a nice automobile like this.

Just then, however, one of the drivers who is talking on his phone loses control of his car. He swerves off the street and—CRASH—runs right into a tree. No one is hurt, thank God, but the car is badly damaged. Steam pours out of the radiator, and fluids leak onto the pavement. It's a mess. Then you have a brainstorm. You can turn your farmland into a factory. Right before your eyes are two products that someone has to make; it might as well be you and your workers.

If you are more inclined to make new parts for wrecked cars, turn to page 109.

On the other hand, everything works with computers. If you think you ought to make the little logic boards that govern these modern machines, turn to page 66.

124

To hide from the British, you flee to a **kibbutz** in the biblical **Wilderness of Zin**. Thirty miles south of **Beersheba, Kibbutz Sde Boker** is about as isolated as a settlement can be. If armed patrols approach this barren territory, they will be seen far away, and you will have enough time to escape into the nearby hills. There, they will never find you.

A short man with a halo of unruly white hair greets you at the dining hall. His appearance is distinctive, but that is not what you notice about him. It is his personality. Almost before he has said *"Shalom"* to you, he has cast his spell. You want to listen to his every word, absorb what he says, follow him and his ideas with hardly a question. His most powerful words gush forth on the subject of *aliyah*. "No Jew can live a full Jewish life outside the Jewish state," he says forcefully. "To live in the **Diaspora** is to live in *galut,* in exile, and that means to disappear as a Jew in a generation or two."

David Ben-Gurion has this forceful magnetic impact on many people. He urges you to study the Arabic language while you are hiding from the British. "Soon," he predicts, "there will be a flood of immigrants into Israel from Arab countries. We shall need people like you to help them settle and make new lives for themselves." And he is right. Within months, Jews from **Yemen, Morocco, Iraq, Egypt**, and many other countries arrive in Israel. They come on planes, on ships, on foot—any way they can. Their former neighbors have made it impossible to continue a secure Jewish life in their homelands; now they must relocate and find safety among other Jews.

If you decide that the best contribution you can make is to help these new Israelis learn Hebrew and find jobs, turn to page 81.

If you are convinced that they must have decent housing, turn to page 24.

125

"Inflation! That's the real problem. Not whether we get ten shekels or twenty shekels, but rising prices. When a **pita** that used to cost half a shekel now costs a full shekel, how can we manage? No one can keep up with those rising prices."

He's right, of course. The problems of inflation are not the fault of a few factory owners or a small group of workers. They are problems for all of Israel, and until they are solved, no company and no family will be financially safe.

The two of you talk late into the night. He tells you that he wants to learn more about how the economy of a country works. "There's only one place to go for this kind of knowledge," you tell him. "That's the **Hebrew University in Jerusalem**. They can teach you how to think like an economist. If that's where you want to go, I can help. I know some of the professors there. We were in the **Haganah** together."

After several years of study, your young friend graduates with a degree in economics. With some of your other connections, you help him find a job with the Israel National Bank (Bank Leumi), and they assign him to a team that works with all elements of Israeli society to control inflation. "If we can help people believe that they will not run out of money and that their salaries will buy the same goods tomorrow as they do today, we can lift these unfair burdens from everyone and eliminate a major cause of conflict in our nation." That you have had a role in leading this young man into such a responsible and important job gives you great satisfaction. You are content.

END

126

A few years pass, and he becomes more aware of the very first **mitzvah** of the Torah, *p'ru urvu,* "be fruitful and multiply" (Genesis 1:28). But he is single, and that is naturally a problem. What to do?

You visit him and suggest that he accompany you to synagogue on **Shabbat** morning. After services, you convince him to tell the rabbi about his problem. "That's easy," the rabbi says, smiling broadly. "We can fix that. Miriam, come over here. Meet some new friends." Winking at you, he introduces a short, energetic, middle-aged woman. "Miriam knows everyone in town. If anyone can find you a wife, it is our *shadchan,* our matchmaker."

While Miriam is trying to arrange a marriage for him, he continues leading the troop of scouts. At one meeting, a young woman who had been a member of the scouts during high school returns from the university for a visit. He looks at her once, then twice. She is now a beautiful adult, and it doesn't take him long to decide what to do. Over the next several months, he visits her at school, and she sees him when she returns home on vacations. By **Shavuot**, he and Ruth are engaged to be married.

The two of them spend the rest of their lives in the very satisfying task of raising their own children and leading the children of their neighbors as scouts. Nothing could make you prouder than to have helped produce these young builders of the Jewish state.

END

127

A shrieking sound interrupts your thoughts. The air-raid alert blares from rooftop speakers, and you immediately turn on the radio. "War has broken out in the region of the **Persian Gulf**," the announcer informs you. "Troops from **Iraq** have invaded **Kuwait**, and we are fairly certain that the enemy will soon turn its attention to us. Everyone knows that they possess rockets with a range long enough to hit Israel. You should at once take precautions to protect yourselves from explosions and from chemical and gas attacks."

You hurry through the crowds to the market at **Machane Yehuda**. On almost every corner, you can buy wide sheets of heavy-duty plastic and tape. You can use these items to cover the door and windows of your apartment; they may not stop everything the Iraqis can rain on you, but they will certainly help. And civil defense workers are passing out gas masks and showing people how to use them. You have to laugh. Your neighbors really look funny in these masks. Of course, you know that it's not really funny. Lots of people could die if they don't use these precautions.

The missiles from **Iraq** hit **Tel Aviv** instead of **Jerusalem**, and you are safe. And even in **Tel Aviv**, the damage is relatively minimal. Then, you understand that no Arab leader would dare to send a missile even close to the **Dome of the Rock** or the **Al-Aqsa Mosque**. If a rocket hit one of these **Islamic** shrines, no one would ever forgive him.

Your city was prepared; now it is safe. You are proud of all the preparations, and you are very grateful that Israel is secure. Peace may be a distant dream, but you are glad that, at least for the moment, you have all been spared.

END

128

Israel is a nation of Jews who have made *aliyah* from every continent, from many, many different lands. Each brought a rich fabric of culture to this new land, but now those varied pieces must become a single patchwork quilt. The tapestry of a unified Israeli culture must be stitched into a common whole that can blanket the entire country.

With others, you decide that there must be a museum that can teach all these various groups about each other. In the process, they will all come to appreciate the richness of Israel's people, and they will begin to create the common culture that will tie these varied new citizens into a unified whole.

Now, you stroll through this new museum that is really a school. Beth Hatefutsoth, the Museum of the **Diaspora**, rises on a hill overlooking **Tel Aviv**. It records the lives of Jews in every part of the world, even **China**. You see groups of soldiers wandering through the hallways, bumping into classes of schoolchildren, and tourists from all over the world. "We are all becoming Israelis," you tell your friends. "We shall not all be alike. Wouldn't it be boring if we were all the same! But we shall all share the experiences that this museum teaches. This will help us become one people."

Only the first steps have been taken toward a unified Israel. But someone had to start. After all, did not the biblical prophet **Joel** [3:1] tell you that even old men have a right to dream dreams. You have had such a vision; you have dreamed such a dream. And now it is becoming a reality. Through all the trials and hardships of your life, maybe it was for this achievement that you were kept alive. "I praise You, God, for helping me survive and for inspiring me and for permitting me to see this special day. Amen."

END

129

The **Palmach** troops defending Jewish **Jerusalem** are desperate for ammunition and weapons. Surrounded on almost every side by the well-armed **Arab Legion**, all they can do is wait and hope for a supply convoy to reach them. If it does not within a few days, they will have to surrender or be killed.

For the supplies to reach **Jerusalem**, however, the trucks must climb a narrow road from **Tel Aviv**. Convoy after convoy has tried to dash past the Arab army's guns, but they have all been destroyed or turned back. The roadside is littered with burned-out trucks. Still, you think, there must be another way.

An American army officer, **Colonel David Marcus**, comes into your camp and seeks out the commander, **Yigael Yadin**. "General," he says, "I have been sneaking around the fortress at **Latrun** on a narrow mountain path. We've gotten foot soldiers up to **Jerusalem** this way, but I suspect that the path might be wide enough for a small truck. Will you give me permission to try? It may be the only way to get what the defenders need into the city."

Yadin has no other choice. In the dark of night, all of you wait in silence, knowing that the trucks are taking an extremely dangerous route. They could fall off a cliff or be captured by the Arabs. But they are not! A green flare arches into the eastern sky, the signal that they have succeeded. It is a miracle!

*You think back to tales you heard as a child about miracles. No! You cannot accept those **Chasidic** legends. But there must be another religious way to respond to the miracle of the **Latrun** Road. If you seek that spiritual path, turn to page 98.*

*If the **Shoah** has made faith in God impossible for you, turn to page 12.*

130

All throughout your life, you have wanted to compose music. Now, toward the end of your life, it is time to indulge this desire. You have a vision of putting your feelings about Israel onto a musical score, setting the many feelings you have about this new land into notes that others can play. Music is, after all, the common language of humanity. If you can fulfill this dream, then every Israeli can experience your inner thoughts and feelings, and musicians can pack the sheet music into their suitcases and carry it throughout the world. Without ever stepping outside your home, you can be an ambassador of Israel and make it possible for knowledge of God's plan to go forth from **Jerusalem** and the word of what has been done in this holy land to emerge from **Zion**.

This is, however, harder than you think. You sit at your piano, tapping out notes, writing them down, then ripping the pages into shreds. Each phrase of music is torture to create, because you are driven to express what you feel in notes that are just right, so close to perfect that no one could do better. You are convinced that God has chosen you to make the dream of Israel come alive through melody, and you cannot stop until your work does honor to the One who commissioned it. What you write must be good enough to tell the world of the destiny of this people, this people committed to God and God's plan in history. Nothing less than this can be sufficient.

You spend the rest of your life working on this project. Sometimes, you produce a piece of music that comes close to the goal. Mostly, you are not satisfied. But after all, you tell yourself, I am only human. I shall do my best, and I pray that my Creator will be satisfied.

END

131

One story follows another, reports that money granted from the government to Shas for its social service projects has been misused. You confront your son-in-law. "Is this happening? Do you know if some of the money that was granted for one purpose has been used for something else? Are you personally involved?"

He responds that it is critical to help the women and children of these poor immigrants, especially the boys who study in the **yeshivot** operated by the political party. "Everyone knows that money is made available for one purpose but diverted to another. They wouldn't give us a grant for the schools, so we had to find a way. That's just the way things are done."

You are worried. It may be that this is "the way things are done," but it's also an illegal way. Yes, it's his decision, and you can only voice your concerns, but it also might affect your daughter and your grandchildren. If something goes wrong, their lives would be changed.

And something does go wrong. He and the others who spent the government money for unauthorized purposes are arrested for misusing public funds. They are convicted in court and sent to prison. His disgrace is a disgrace for your entire family. Your daughter and her children move in with you and your wife. At least this is a good outcome. You now have a chance to teach these wonderful grandchildren about right and wrong. Perhaps you can raise them so that they will not make the same mistakes that their father did.

END

132

Y our daughter stands by the side of the road, the road that Arab workers from **Gaza** use every day to drive to their jobs in Israel. Unfortunately, there have been a number of fatal car crashes on this road. On one side of the border, a group of nervous Israeli women shift their weight from foot to foot. On the other side, a similar group of Arab women glare suspiciously at the Israelis.

Your daughter speaks. "I think it is time for us, women whose husbands and brothers are dying on this road, to stop the slaughter. My interns and I have gotten the Israeli and the Palestinian police, the insurance companies, and the taxi drivers to contribute to a fund. We have bought reflectors and other safety devices that will help reduce the number of accidents. A worker coming back to **Gaza** in the dark after a long working day needs all the help he can get. Together, we can provide that help."

Conversation breaks out within each group of women. You know they are debating whether to help each other. Then one Palestinian woman steps forward. "I am willing to work with you. If they want to help save the lives of my husband and my son, who am I to stand in the way? Let the project begin."

The reflector buttons are nailed to trees and posts. Reflecting paint is daubed on rocks and curbs. "We'll get some of the men with heavy painting machines to put stripes down the side of the road," women from both communities agree.

At the end of the day, a small project, but an important step has been completed. Peace is not yet a reality, but, you all conclude, *shalom* is achieved one step at a time.

END

133

You are sure that the rabbinate will decide in favor of these immigrants, but to your surprise, the opposite happens. "We cannot be sure that their conversions were legal according to Jewish tradition. Someone cannot become Jewish without the proper ritual conducted by the proper authorities. If we allow these people to claim being Jewish, there might be other groups that would make similar, false claims."

"Now the truth is out," you think to yourself. "The **Orthodox** rabbinate must protect its monopoly on conversion. If they accept these **African Hebrew Israelites** as Jews, they might have to accept converts from **Reform** or Conservative Judaism. This is the real root of their objection."

To the general climate of defensiveness and suspicion that has grown up around **Dimona**'s nuclear reactor has been added the conflict between the **Orthodox** rabbinate and liberal Jews in Israel.

After the hatred and prejudice you experienced during the war, you cannot accept this kind of conflict and division. You recall that **Amos** said that Israelites and Ethiopians were the same in God's sight [9:7]. Surely, this universal value has not changed. The ideas first expressed in the Bible must still be true.

To rekindle some of these ideas in your own thinking, turn to page 135.

134

Your granddaughter is entranced by the music of the Jewish people, especially the music that comes out of the *shtetlach* of Eastern Europe, from the time when Jewish culture was vibrant and active, from before the war. Every evening, she and her friends gather in someone's home to listen to tapes of old records. They find themselves tapping their feet and smiling together, and soon they agree that they ought to try to play some of these tunes themselves.

The **klezmer** band they form finds almost instant popularity. People love this happy and upbeat music. They are asked to play at all sorts of celebrations and festivals, and they accept as many of the invitations as possible. It's not just music, they tell you; it's our music, the music of our people, and we are keeping it alive.

At a wedding one evening, they are playing a *freilach* when an old man approaches your granddaughter. He holds in his hand a violin case, scratched and battered, but still intact. "I came from **Russia**," he says. "We couldn't take many possessions with us, but I just could not leave this instrument behind. Now, my fingers are too stiff to play. But you make the beautiful sounds of my youth. I want you to have this violin."

Your granddaughter tries to refuse this generous gift, but he insists. "You must have it." As she places the rest under her chin, gently fingers the frets, and places the bow on the strings, a great sense of joy comes over her. The past of the Jewish people is coming alive through her. She and everyone around her know that the sound is the magic of the Jewish people and its survival. And now it is no longer the sound of the Jewish past; it is the sound of tomorrow.

END

135

Y ou have always loved listening to the stories of the early chapters of Genesis. When the Torah was chanted and translated during services in the synagogue, you pretended in your own mind that you were Noah, **Abraham and Sarah**, and Joseph. From each of these ancient tales, you learned basic truths, and you have never had any reason to turn from them.

One of the lessons you learned from Genesis is that people have an obligation to take care of the earth [Genesis 1:28 and 2:15]. And if that is true about soil and air and water and plants, shouldn't it be even more true about people? After all, another Genesis story tells about Cain, who murdered his brother, Abel. When God called out to him, asking where Abel was, Cain answered, "Am I my brother's keeper?" [4:9]. The answer did not even need to be written down: "Of course you are!"

When you look in the newspaper, you see photographs of Black people in **Africa**, starving, dying, suffering because their crops have failed. Looking at these photographs makes you think about the truths of Judaism that you learned so long ago from the Book of Genesis. If you are to be faithful to what you think it means to be a Jew, you must find a way to help them.

*If you agree to join a team of Israeli experts in central **Africa**, turn to page 21.*

If you decide to continue building up the Land of Israel, turn to page 40.

136

The day has been confusing and troubling for you. As you walk home, one thought after another rushes into your head. "How can these **Chasidim** believe that they have the only truth? Couldn't someone else be right? The Torah does say that one must not do any work on the Sabbath day. Today is **Shabbat**. Maybe the stone throwers were right to protest this violation of religious law. Israel is made up of lots of different kinds of Jews. There must be a way to find peace among them. But peace that means accepting working on **Shabbat**. Why would anyone choose to make that compromise?"

Sitting in your living room, you watch the sun setting over the **Dome of the Rock**. "We have enough trouble living next to our **Moslem** and Arab neighbors. Can't we live in peace with other Jews?" That's a good question, but a larger issue troubles you. Maybe the **Chasidim** are, in fact, right. You are completely confused, not at all sure of what you believe. You walk back and forth in your apartment, pacing, your hands in your pockets. Hello! What's this? A piece of paper, something one of the rioters handed you earlier in the afternoon.

The paper is really a message from the *rebbe*. You read it and something calming and secure touches you. You understand for the first time that he is right, that there is only one way—his way, the Torah's way, God's way. You become a *baal t'shuvah* and spend the rest of your days studying in a **yeshivah**. This, you conclude, is the way God has meant you to live. You feel that you have chosen a right and good path.

END

137

You admire the power of the certainty. It must be wonderful to be so completely sure of what you believe. Yes, their way of life forces them to separate from the rest of society, to live in a different way; but they don't consider this a sacrifice. To them, living in the way of Torah is living in the way that, they believe, God commanded them.

It may be all right for them, but it cannot be right for you. You wish you could have their strength of faith and simple conviction that God controls all human events. But their God did not save your family from the Holocaust. If there is such a God as they claim, where was this God at **Auschwitz** and **Bergen-Belsen**? They may believe with perfect faith; you cannot, as hard as you try.

What sustains you, what keeps you going is memory. Memory and the knowledge that the enemies of the Jews all failed to destroy us, while we continue as a living people. To keep these memories alive becomes your reason for living. You become a volunteer at the house of memory, at **Yad Vashem**, the Holocaust Memorial Center. You may no longer go to a synagogue, but this sacred place is, in fact, better for you than any synagogue. In keeping the memories alive, you feel you are doing a holy task. And what could give more meaning to your life than this?

END

138

Your son-in-law calls a family meeting. "I have just discovered that some of my fellow Shas members have taken money from one program and used it for another. This is not right. They tell me that it's for a good purpose and that 'the end justifies the means,' but I don't believe that. I cannot accept the idea that politicians will all be thought of as crooks. Someone must demonstrate that it is honorable to enter public service, that one can work for the good of the people and also be honest."

What a statement! You beam with joy when you hear your daughter's husband say this. And you realize that your grandchildren will grow up in a home where the right values are put into practice, where their parents will give them models of behaving in ethical and moral ways.

You are not surprised to discover that he has entered his name on the Shas list of candidates for the **Knesset**, Israel's parliament. It's the obvious consequence of what he had said at the family meeting. And you are not surprised when he is elected.

He keeps his promise to be ethical and is reelected over and over again. You sit with your daughter and your grandchildren in the balcony of the **Knesset** chamber and watch as he is sworn in for the fourth time, this time also as a cabinet minister in the government. You were an immigrant from Europe; he was an immigrant from **Morocco**. But both of you have had major roles in building the new State of Israel. After the swearing-in ceremony, you embrace. You are both very proud of your lives.

END

139

As you land at Ben-Gurion Airport, you realize that you have now lived in Eastern Europe twice and you have entered Israel twice. But the Jewish Eastern Europe you lived in the second time was altogether different from the *shtetl* communities you experienced as a child. That civilization is no more; the **Nazis** and their allies destroyed it so completely that it can never be re-created.

Or can it? It dawns on you that young **sabras** will never know about the richness of prewar Eastern Europe unless somehow it can be reborn and brought back to life for them. Some of them think that the Jews of Eastern Europe had no music and no theater and no businesses and no schools—they were just weak Jews who lacked the courage to stand up to the Germans. Had they lived in Israel, these young Israelis believe, they would have been strong and vital and admirable.

How wrong they are! Yes, the Jews of Eastern Europe were different from the modern young Jews you know in Israel, but they were not weak or worthless. They kept Judaism alive for centuries when there was no Israel, when no one even dreamed seriously of reestablishing the Jewish state. Today's young Israelis need to know this history.

You become a guide at the new Beth Hatefutsoth. Many groups of schoolchildren and new soldiers in the army visit the Museum of the Diaspora, and you tell them about the strengths and contributions of Jews who lived throughout the world. Dedicating your life to this pursuit gives you great satisfaction. You are remembering the past, but you are also building a solid foundation for the new country.

END

140

After you arrive in Israel, you go to visit **Jerusalem**. While you are there, you meet some of the *olim* you had helped in **Russia**. They put their arms around your shoulders and propel you toward the ancient **Temple Mount** in the center of biblical **Jerusalem**. "Look," one of them points. "Do you see that archaeological dig? The one at the south end of the Mount, near the wide steps?"

You see dozens of Israeli students, led by their professors, carefully sifting through the dirt and slowly digging their way down through the centuries. "Can't you see?" your Russian friend says. "For years we were forbidden to study Jewish history. We had no idea of our past, where we came from, the stories of the Bible and the Rabbis, how we survived from **Sinai** until today. Now, we are actually uncovering ancient pieces of pottery and stone. They tell our story. And with them come religious ideas that are as true today as they were thousands of years ago. This is truly a miracle."

He's right. It is a miracle. An entire generation of Jews who were about to die as Jews have been brought back to life. Here in Israel, they have discovered the excitement of their heritage and their people. And you and your colleagues in **Russia** helped make it happen. If all you had accomplished in your life was this, *dayeinu*, it would have been enough.

END

141

In biblical times, the cities of **Sodom** and **Gomorrah** at the south end of the **Dead Sea** were places of exceptional evil. They were so bad that God destroyed them with a fiery lightning bolt. "Now," the young doctor of electricity suggests, "we can turn the power of this region into something positive. There has been a lot of destruction in this desert. It's time that we built something good down here."

Even though **Jordan** and Israel are technically at war with each other, she arranges a meeting with a group of engineers from that country. They meet in the resort town of **Eilat**, where they can relax together, become friends, and share their ideas about engineering and electricity. Sometimes they walk across the border into the Jordanian town of **Aqaba**. "Wouldn't it be great if we could cooperate on some project as easily as we can sit in a café and drink coffee together?" one of the Jordanian engineers muses.

"You've given me an idea," she responds. "Up in the **Arava**, right where **Sodom** used to be, there is nothing on the ground. But in the sky there is always a burning sun. We all know about solar power. Could we not figure out how to harness that energy in a joint project that would benefit both of our countries? It would work. All we have to do is convince the politicians that it is a good thing to do."

Easier said than done. But an immigrant woman from a traditional society who has earned a doctorate in engineering is nothing if not determined. She enlists you and many others in the pursuit of this project, and eventually you get the green light. As the first surge of power flows into both countries from the solar collectors, you are overjoyed to have helped build a network of power for peace, not for war.

END

142

This former student of yours sits in your living room, swirling the deep brown tea around the bottom of her cup. "Look at this tea! If we did not have water, we could not have brewed it. Water is the key to the future of Israel. You know that we have only one source of fresh water, the streams that feed into the **Kinneret**. But there is only a limited amount of water in them, and everyone wants it. There simply will not be enough water to go around in the future . . . unless we do something daring."

"What would that daring act be?" you ask her, knowing that she already has an idea in mind. "When I was studying at the university, we passed an electrical current through salt water. We were able to separate the salt molecules from the rest of the liquid and that remainder was as fresh as the water of the **Banias Falls**. That was a little experiment in our lab. If we could do the same thing on a much bigger scale, I think we could solve Israel's water shortage."

You agree that it might be worth a try, and the next thing you hear is that she has formed a team and established a pilot project of desalinization of seawater. Israel has lots of salt water, so the raw materials are available. She has, so far, had only limited success, but she will not quit. The future of the Jewish state depends, she says, on the success of her project, and knowing her, you bet she will overcome all obstacles and succeed.

END

143

Some Russian Jews will not leave their homeland. They fear the anti-Semitism that is everywhere in their country, but they love the sound of the language, the beauty of the sights, the smells of the food . . . this is their home, and they are not prepared to abandon all those special things with which they have grown up.

Staying in **Russia**, however, presents them with a problem. For over seventy years, the **Communist** government has made being Jewish very difficult, often almost a criminal offense. There certainly was no Jewish or Hebrew education available, and only the very oldest people remember a time when Judaism could be practiced openly and with dignity. For most of their lives, these people have experienced being Jewish as something dangerous. If you were openly Jewish, you could be fired from your job, kicked out of the university, forced to move from your apartment. If the government wanted, it could arrest you and send you to a prison camp in **Siberia** for years of hard labor. You might never return.

Now, it is true, the Russian Jews can be openly Jewish. But the old fears still persist. And they have no background that will help them decide what kind of a Jewish person to be, now that some measure of freedom and choice is available. You talk to some of the older people, and they suggest you lead the younger Jews of **Russia** in one of two paths.

If you think they should choose a traditional style of Jewish life, turn to page 44.

If, on the other hand, you think they would do better with a liberal style of Jewish life, turn to page 27.

144

Whether they come to **Eilat** for business or pleasure, people have to have somewhere to sleep. That's for sure. You open a hotel, just a few blocks to the south of town, along the harbor. Your guests can sit on the terrace in the morning and have breakfast overlooking the hills of **Jordan** amidst the commotion of a busy port. At night, the band you have engaged helps them finish their day with dancing and fun.

From your hotel, your guests can walk into town to see the sights or take a quick boat ride down the gulf to the reefs. With the help of a friendly Jordanian border policeman, you can even arrange Jeep tours into the desert, all the way to the **Nabatean** city of red rocks, **Petra**. It's one of the wonders of the world, and you recommend it to all your guests.

One day, after the tourists have left for their diving and the business people have gone into town, you settle into a chair for your own breakfast. As you lift your cup of coffee, your hand trembles. You look at the headline in the newspaper, and you are shocked. It seems that the Israeli and Egyptian governments are discussing the future of the coastline near **Taba**, just down the Egyptian shore of the gulf from **Eilat**. It seems that this region, Israeli since the 1967 war, might be returned to **Egypt**. But this is the place where your boat lands. Without **Taba**, all your seagoing trips will be impossible; without **Taba**, your business will be destroyed. You cannot believe that your own government would stab you in the back in this way.

*If you decide to abandon **Eilat** and move back to
Tel Aviv, turn to page 65.*

*If, on the other hand, you analyze the situation and
decide to make the best of it, turn to page 170.*

145

They had always visualized diamonds set in engagement rings, placed lovingly on the fingers of blushing, smiling women in love by men who adore them. Now, a different reality sets in. The diamonds your daughter is supposed to sell are not big stones for jewelry, but little fragments, almost dust, that will be used for drill bits in industrial machines. The diamond dust is so hard that these drills will be able to cut through almost any other material.

It's a mystery to her. What do the drills actually do once they are made? Do they manufacture weapons of war or computers or what? On a vacation drive through the **Arava** on the way to the resort of **Eilat**, your daughter and her family are amazed to see green fields. "How can they possibly grow crops out here in the dry desert? Where do they get the water?"

They stop and visit **Kibbutz Lotan** and meet its manager. "The water comes through tunnels. Years ago this would not have been possible. But now we can drill these holes with drills tipped with diamond dust. It makes it possible for us to cultivate our vegetable crops, even out here."

When they return to **Haifa**, your grandchildren bound into your apartment and spill their special news. "Did you know, *Saba*, that *Abba* and *Ima* sold the diamonds that made the drills that made the holes that made the crops that made the desert green? Look, we brought you some flowers from **Lotan**. Aren't you proud that your daughter helped made this part of Israel come alive?"

And you are . . . very proud indeed.

END

146

There's no romance in the diamond business at all. People don't really trust each other. They are hard and cynical. Money seems to be everything. Your daughter and her husband make lots of money. Are they happy? Well, usually. But occasionally, they wonder; they doubt whether all the things they can buy with their money are enough to make life worthwhile. Most of the time the doubts pass, but not always.

One day—it's not a special day of any sort, just a day—your son-in-law calls and asks you and your wife to come for dinner. Nothing unusual here. You go to their house often. But when you come in, you notice something a little strange. The table has a fancy cloth on it; there are flowers in every vase; your daughter has one of her nicer dresses on, and your son-in-law is even wearing a tie.

"What's going on here? Is this a party of some sort?" "No, *Abba*, no party. But you're right. Today is special. You and *Ima* got married when you were young and poor. You were never able to give her a nice diamond ring. We know she wants one, so here, here is a ring we got from our friends in **Holland**. Give it to *Ima*. You've been in love with each other for so many years. Now, you'll be able to make her even happier."

Tears flow from your eyes as you embrace your children. Despite the toughness of their business, they still understand romance. How could you be more grateful to them than you are right now? But another surprise awaits. At dinner, your daughter stands up. "This is just about the last time I'll be able to wear this dress for a while. You are going to be grandparents. You see, we too still know what romance is all about!"

Your life is full. You are enormously content with your lot in life.

END

147

After the ceremony, you and your family visit the cave where Shimon bar Yochai and his son, Eleazar, supposedly hid from Roman soldiers for twelve years. It was during this time, tradition teaches, that he began collecting material for the **Mishnah**, and some of his **midrashim** have survived to our day. Some **kabbalists** believe that he was the original author of the *Zohar*, the mystical book that contains the secrets of the universe. Did a miracle happen in this cave? Ha! You suspect he and his son went a little nuts living in a dark, damp cave for such a long time.

Then, a strange but wonderful thing happens. As you sit on the hillside, eating a picnic lunch, you and your family begin to share stories of miracles that have happened to you. Your son-in-law tells you about a time when he was unhappy with his job, but the boss "miraculously" gave him a promotion. Your wife recalls how she was "miraculously" cured from very bad headaches. Even you have to admit that your survival in the concentration camps was something like a miracle. For the first time in many years, all of you are talking in a new way. There is friendly communication and understanding within the family. Is this a modern miracle?

You don't know, but would it hurt to end such a special day with a prayer? *Baruch atah Adonai asher g'malanu kol tov*, "Praised are You, Eternal One, who has done so many good things for all of us." Amen.

END

148

Glueck shares his dream with you. "In the **United States**, where I live, if something is two hundred years old, it is very ancient. Our society is so new that we don't really understand what it means to survive for three thousand years. If young Jews are to appreciate the gift that Judaism is for them, they must learn how their heritage goes directly back to the days of **Abraham and Sarah**, all the way back in an unbroken chain to the time of the Bible. The best way for them to understand this is by digging through their people's past."

There is already a school in the eastern section of **Jerusalem** named after **William Albright**, one of **Glueck**'s teachers. But the **American School of Oriental Research** is in the Arab section of the city, an area not open to Jewish students. **Glueck** dreams of founding a similar archaeological research school in the Jewish part of the city. His eyebrows arch. "I want every Jewish student to experience the glory of the Jewish past. I want them to see pots and statues and lamps that our biblical ancestors actually used. I want them to share the enthusiasm for the Jewish past and the tradition that grew out of it that I find so exciting." As he speaks, he fondles a small jug, and you can actually imagine with him that **Moses** himself might have had a drink of water from this simple clay container.

*If you join **Glueck** in trying to achieve his vision, turn to page 63.*

If, on the other hand, you want to skip the last several thousand years and return to the concerns of the modern world, turn to page 43.

149

Theodor Herzl had once considered the island of **Cyprus** as an alternative to a Jewish national homeland in Palestine. But the plan was rejected, as were similar schemes to resettle European Jews in the **El-Arish** region of northern **Egypt** and in **Uganda**. Nothing but the historical region of **Zion** would be acceptable.

Now, you and about 26,000 other Jewish refugees are detained in two camps on that same island. The conditions are terrible. It is hot and crowded, the food is awful, and medical care is barely adequate. "Soon, we shall be able to go to Palestine," you tell each other, encouraging hope and optimism. Classes in spoken Hebrew are organized by some of the refugees who have more language skills than others, and representatives of the **Jewish Agency** and other Jewish welfare organizations arrange for entertainment and discussions to pass the time.

When Israel's independence becomes a reality in May 1948, you are instantly ready to hop on a ship. Unfortunately, there are few transports available, and it is not until September that the first refugees are transported to **Haifa**. You are among those who leave first, because you are an able-bodied man, and Israel needs you to fight against the Arabs.

When the armistice is declared, you have a decision to make.

If you decide that you must continue your education, turn to page 164.

But, if you are determined that you will never again be poor, turn to page 165.

150

There's no question in your mind that a major threat to Israel is the combined armies of the neighboring Arab countries. They outnumber the military of the new and tiny Jewish nation many times. But you become convinced that the best way to resist their assaults will be to know what they intend to do before they actually do it.

You enlist in Israel's clandestine military intelligence service, the **Shin Bet**. Soon, you find yourself traveling outside the country, consulting with other intelligence services, like the American Federal Bureau of Investigation (FBI). You share information with their agents . . . but, of course, there are some secrets you cannot tell, even to your country's friends.

As the little bits of information add up to a bigger picture, you understand that there are really two dangers.

On the one hand, small groups of enemy guerillas will try to cross the northern border of Israel from **Lebanon** and **Syria**. They can do a great deal of damage in the new settlements of the **Galilee**. If you decide to try to stop them, turn to page 94.

Many Arabs fled to neighboring countries when Israel declared its independence. They had assumed that the Arab armies would easily defeat the Jews and that they would be able to return in triumph. Now, they are refugees. But a large number of Arabs stayed in the new country. Is it possible that they, too, are allied with the enemies of the state?

To find out, turn to page 95.

151

On **Shabbat** morning, you listen as the story of the **Exodus** from **Egypt** unfolds once again in the synagogue. If the Torah is anywhere near correct, there was a huge group that fled Egyptian slavery—603,500 men, plus their wives, children, some non-Israelite people who came along, and all their cattle. From this account, you conclude that the total must have been three or four million people.

How, you wonder, did they feed themselves during the forty years of wandering through the desert? You've been down to this region yourself. Hardly anything grows there now. Just a few thorny bushes. Most of the ground is sandy, and you think God must have had an extra supply of rocks that were deposited in the **Sinai**. It would be hard to imagine how anything could grow in this wasteland, but it must have been different in ancient times. That's the only way you can make sense of the biblical account; this desert was not always a desert! People once knew how to make the barren soil yield crops for food.

If it could have happened three thousand years ago, it could probably happen today. The sterile slopes of **Judea** and the **Sinai** could be brought back to life. And if you can learn how to do it there, then you might be able to apply the same skills and techniques to **sub-Saharan Africa**. Then, one individual— or a small army of individuals—could move around in that region of the world and make a huge difference.

*You decide to test your theories near the biblical city of **Sodom**. Turn to page 77.*

*Another way to proceed is to experiment in an area just south of the city of **Jericho**. To do that, turn to page 6.*

152

As you crouch over the archaeological dig with your daughter, a shadow falls over you. How strange! There are no trees here, nor are there roads where there could be vehicles. What is this shadow?

You turn slowly around and come face to face with four very large men in long black coats, with huge beards, and fur-trimmed black hats. "It is forbidden by Jewish law to dig at this place," one of them says sternly. "You may not disturb this ground, where Jews from generations past may lie in their eternal homes."

He is not prepared for your daughter's response. She stands up, not nearly as tall as he is, but just as firm. "What do you know about this site? Have you seen any bones, any coffins, any indication that it might even possibly be a cemetery? Please, if you have any evidence, present it to me now. And if you do not, I shall have to ask you to leave. This place is special. I respect it immensely. But it is not a cemetery. It is a place of dirt and ashes and stones—and a place of very important memories. Now, show me evidence or go!"

He does not know what to do, how to react to a woman who speaks to him so strongly. So he and his friends do the only thing they can. They turn abruptly and stomp away, grumbling in their beards about modern women and modern life.

You realize that these men represent a different way of seeing the world. You certainly do not agree with them, but you understand that their perspective is light-years away from yours. You hope that, even though there are such differences, you could disagree with *menschlichkeit*. Of course, you doubt that they will ever respect your point of view, but that is, after all, modern Israel, and for better or for worse, you love it.

END

153

After Israel's stunning victory over the combined Arab armies in 1948, the lives of nearly 2,500,000 Jews living in those regions have become difficult and dangerous. Bands of **Moslem** rioters swarm through the Jewish quarters of many cities, destroying Jewish homes and businesses and harassing Jews themselves. It is clear to everyone that these Jews can no longer stay in the countries where they and their ancestors had lived for more than a thousand years.

The Jews of **Yemen** and **South Aden** are among those most seriously affected. Something must be done to rescue these 50,000 members of your people, to bring them to Israel and give them a safe new life. In a **Joint Distribution Committee** camp, they gather, having struggled by foot across many miles of rugged terrain. Of course, you know that it took many bribes to convince the rulers of this region to prevent their armies from attacking the refugee columns. Had that happened, the massacre would have been total.

Unmarked DC-4s land near the camp and seat up to 200 Yemenite Jews on the floor of each airplane. Shuttling back and forth up to eight times each day, **Operation Magic Carpet** brings all the Jews of southern **Arabia** to Israel. There, in resettlement centers, they are given decent housing and food, taught elementary Hebrew, and prepared for a new life in the Jewish state.

Continue on page 185.

154

With **Eban**, you have seen again how important it is to give impoverished and desperate people skills to help themselves. But that's nothing new to you. The **Babylonian Talmud** [*Kiddushin* 29a] taught you that it is a father's obligation to teach his son a trade, and **Moses Maimonides** held that the highest form of charity is to give others the ability to support themselves. Now, you decide that it will be your life's work to carry out this **mitzvah**.

On an outing with your family and friends to **Masada**, you spend a little too much time in the sun. The burn on your skin is painful, but it reminds you that Israel has a major natural resource—sunlight. The power of the sun, if you could harness it, could be a real light to the nations. If you could find a way to share solar power with countries that do not have waterfalls or oil or coal, you could, indeed, be *l'or goyim*, "a light to the nations" [Isaiah 42:6].

You turn to the professors at the **Technion**, the old technical university in **Haifa**. They, too, become energized by the project, but they ask you a question: "Do you think it will be more important to develop something we can use in Israel, or is your goal to invent something that will be applied elsewhere?"

If your intention is to take the new idea to other countries, turn to page 49.

On the other hand, if this is a project that will be important in Israel, turn to page 167.

155

The Israeli ambassador to the United Nations rises to speak. "There are some today who say that Israel has developed an atomic bomb, a weapon capable of destroying masses of people. I am here to tell you that this is not true. My country does not have such a destructive weapon that it could use today or tomorrow. We do not!"

Of course, he did not say "the day after tomorrow." A former scientist who worked at the **Dimona** laboratory has told a reporter from the *New York Times* that Israel does have nuclear military weapons. "We are a very small country. We are surrounded by hostile Arab nations with large armies and lots of money from the sale of oil. This money can be used to purchase all sorts of weapons that could be used to destroy us. **Iraq** in particular is known to have stockpiles of weapons of mass destruction. Would it not be reckless and stupid of us not to create similar weapons to protect ourselves?"

Within a few days after this article appears, **Shin Bet** agents swoop down on his **Dimona** home and arrest this scientist. "He has blurted out important, secret military information. This is treason against Israel. He has done more damage to our country than the very weapons he claims the Arabs have." The security agents are furious.

*So are you, but for different reasons. If you are upset because you believe the **Shin Bet**'s claim that this man has injured Israel's ability to defend itself,* *turn to page 50.*

On the other hand, if you are outraged that Israel has joined the exclusive club of nations that have atomic bombs, *turn to page 80.*

156

Brother Daniel must have found something very attractive in the Catholic religion for him to have remained a monk after the war. You wonder what that special quality is. At his invitation, you come to the Carmelite monastery in **Haifa** for a weekend retreat. Perhaps if you live among the monks for a few days, you will get some idea of what drew him into their community and persuaded him to devote the rest of his life to this faith.

You attend services with the monks, eat in their dining hall, and share their daily chores. On **Shabbat**, they are gracious enough not to ask you to work, even though they are out in the gardens, hoeing and raking and planting new flowers. "Maybe," you think to yourself, "it is this respect for someone else's religion that he found so endearing. Or maybe it's their total and absolute commitment to their religion that makes them so special."

As you pack to leave his monastery, Brother Daniel shakes your hand. "I know you are searching for your own spiritual path. I pray that you will find it. There are Jewish roads to God that are just as holy as my Catholic way. You must seek one of them, and then you will find peace . . . peace within yourself and peace for your family."

The door slams behind you with a loud bang. You will never again return to this place, but it will always be with you. Brother Daniel was right. There are Jewish ways to find internal peace, and there are Jewish roads that lead to God. You will spend the rest of your life searching for just the right one. And the search itself, surprisingly, will be what brings you peace. *Shalom!*

END

157

The situation is desperate. The Israeli army lacks almost everything needed to defend the new country. There are barely enough guns—most of them rather old and small—and even these lack ammunition. The artillery, tanks, and airplanes are pitifully inadequate, especially in the face of the combined armies of Israel's Arab neighbors.

The youthful commander of the army, General **Yigael Yadin**, sends for you. "You know how to deal with people in Eastern Europe. That's where you come from. I want you to travel to **Czechoslovakia** for us. In **Prague**, you will meet with representatives of the Czech arms industry. It is possible that they will sell us the guns and bullets we need. A lot depends on you, but don't worry. While you are in **Prague**, others are in the **United States**, arranging for secret shipments of weapons. One way or another, we shall defend ourselves."

You undertake this important mission and are successful. The Czechs have a long history of compassion toward war refugees, and besides, they will get paid for their guns in U.S. dollars. Weapons from the Czech factory at Skoda are secretly unloaded at Israeli ports and soon turn the tide of battle. Within a few months, Israel is in a safer position, and a nervous truce is declared.

If your experiences in Israel's armed forces have convinced you that the future security of the country depends on an air force, turn to page 14.

But, if you think that Israel will be best defended by knowing what its enemies are plotting, turn to page 150.

158

Y ou and your wife don't notice at first, but soon it seems that your handsome son is spending a lot of time working in the same area as a certain young woman. As the saying goes, "it doesn't take a rocket scientist" to figure out that they are growing very fond of each other. And then it becomes obvious that they have fallen deeply in love. One **Shabbat** evening, after *Kiddush* has been chanted in the dining hall and the **challah** has been broken, they lean across the table and tell you that they want to be married. Your tears and hugs and kisses attract everyone's attention, and soon the entire **kibbutz** is singing *siman tov u-mazal tov*, "congratulations and good luck," at the top of their lungs.

But the rabbi of **Yahel** is forbidden to perform the wedding. He is a **Reform** Jewish rabbi, and in Israel only the official rabbis of the **Orthodox** Chief Rabbi's office are allowed by law to marry couples. "This isn't fair," the bride and the groom complain. "We know our rabbi; we haven't even seen the other person. And we're **Reform**, not **Orthodox**. Why can't we have a wedding with the person we know in the style of Judaism we actually practice and enjoy?"

You agree that it's not fair and it's not right and it's not a lot of things, but that's the way Israeli law is. If they want to get married in Israel, they will have to go along with the system.

*If they agree to have an official **Orthodox** wedding, turn to page 96.*

If they can't accept that restriction and find another way to wed, turn to page 41.

159

Y ou rent a room in the home of German Jews who now live in the Carmel section of **Haifa**. The next evening, there is a meeting of the residents of this neighborhood, and you attend. Seated behind the speaker is a short woman. Just looking at her, you get a sense of strength and energy, so after the meeting, you introduce yourself. "I suppose I should know who you are, but I got off the boat, joined the *Irgun*, and am only now learning about Israel. Who are you?"

"My name is Golda, **Golda Meir**."

"Well, perhaps you can answer my question. I want to help this new country grow. What should I do?"

"It's very simple," she replies. "Yes, we shall need a strong military force to fight off the Arab nations. But our real strength will be our people, working people, who create factories and build things, people who go to university and become scientists and teachers, people who help immigrants like yourself become productive citizens of Israel. In the long run, it is the people who will make Israel strong."

Mrs. Meir arranges for you to take a job with the Ministry of Labor, and you enjoy helping workers gain in skill and knowledge. This will strengthen Israel. Soon, two new opportunities present themselves.

One possibility is to help bring even more immigrants to Israel. If you think that might be the right choice, turn to page 101.

*If, however, you accept **Mrs. Meir**'s invitation to go on a diplomatic mission with her, turn to page 102.*

Fruitful crops have been grown in the northern valleys of Israel since biblical times. From the **Jezreel** and the **Sharon**, ancient Israelites harvested grain and raised their flocks. Had it not been for these fertile areas, no prophets would have spoken of justice and right, no priests would have offered sacrifices to God, no kings would have been able to lead their armies into battle.

Near the town of **Afula** in the **Sharon Valley**, there is a section of land that is unused. It is owned by a rich man in **Beirut,** but he is willing to sell it to the **Jewish National Fund (JNF)**, which acquires land in the new country and rents it out for appropriate purposes. To be sure, the absentee landlord exacts a high price, but you know that Israel must take possession of all of its territory.

On this land, you sow crops of barley and plant row upon row of vegetables. Onions and leeks and cabbages sprout quickly in the rich soil, while white-blossomed almond trees and ancient olive trees line the edges of the acres you are allowed to use. Once the vegetable crops are harvested, you turn to the grain. Each year seems to bring a better harvest. As you sit in your sukkah, you and your family sing psalms of praise to God for having blessed you with such a bounty.

*As she grows up, your daughter attends high school in **Afula**. One day, she comes home and asks your permission to take a field trip with her class. They are going, she explains, to visit a famous archaeological site. If you give her permission, turn to page 122.*

If you begin to have trouble with your farm and wonder if you should continue raising crops, turn to page 123.

161

From the moment that you embarked on that rusty ship in **Italy** and made the illegal trip across the **Mediterranean** to Israel, you have been in love with the sea. There is something magical and soothing that you find just watching the waves curl up on the beach or walking with your bare feet in the surf. Yes, you've got to do something in **Eilat** that has to do with the sea.

With money that you borrow from some friends, you purchase a boat and diving equipment. Some Israelis come from the northern region of the country for their vacations, but many more tourists arrive from Northern Europe from countries like **Sweden, Germany**, and **Switzerland**. Some are Jews, but mostly they are not Jewish. All of these diverse people have come for just one reason, to share the sun and the sea, to have a good time, to rest and to enjoy themselves.

You notice something very special. On your boat, everyone cooperates. They may be very different people on land, but on the boat they are all the same. In fact, they enjoy getting to know each other. You meet a tourist from **England** who is a rabbi, though in his bathing suit he doesn't look much like a rabbi. He reminds you of an old rabbinic **midrash**. It tells of two fishermen in a boat. While they are sitting in the middle of the lake, one pulls out a drill and starts to make a hole in the bottom of the boat. "What are you doing?" cries his friend. "Oh, don't worry! I'm only drilling under my own seat!"

In your boat, there is no such thing as "one's own seat." Everyone is there together, having fun, getting acquainted. You have found a way to make Israel a place where different people can get to know each other and become friends. This is the **mitzvah** for which you want to be remembered.

END

162

The negotiating team for the companies offers a modest raise. They tell the workers, "We know that you need more money. The cost of living has gone up five percent, so we are willing to pay you that much more. A five-percent raise will protect you from inflation."

But that simply keeps the workers even. It does not give them a real increase. And that is not what they had in mind. All the families need more shekels to pay their rent and buy food, clothing, school supplies, and everything else. The workers' committee tells the bosses that their offer is inadequate, but the companies are unwilling to increase it. There seems to be no alternative but a strike.

At the aircraft plant, the strike drags on and on. Finally, the company raises its offer a little, and the workers, who desperately need to go back to work and earn their wages, agree. It's a strike that has accomplished very little.

But at the little computer assembly plant, it's a different story. One of the workers gets a bright idea. "Instead of working for this company, let's make an offer. We can try to buy the company, become partners, and work for ourselves. I bet the Histadrut would even help us with a loan for the down payment."

He's right! Eight of the workers become owners of their own business. It's an impossible dream, but it has come true. "Here we are," they exclaim as they raise a **Kiddush** cup and recite a **b'rachah**. "Just a few years ago, we were penniless immigrants. Now we are owners. What a wonderful country Israel is!"

END

163

The British warship comes closer and closer. The *Exodus* is trapped between an armed pursuer and the sandy shore; soon, it will run aground, and all aboard will be taken prisoner. You decide that your dreams for a free future will not end this way. Grabbing a life preserver, you leap over the side rail and into the **Mediterranean**. Because the British are concentrating so hard on the *Exodus*, they fail to see you. The sea is calm, and you swim the half mile to the beach easily.

A group of Palestinian Jews on shore have been following the dramatic offshore chase. They quickly wrap you in a blanket and move you into the city of **Haifa**, where, among the many thousands of other people, you will not be discovered.

For the next several days, you learn everything you can about the *yishuv*. Your future life will very much depend on what choices you make. At night, you sit up late with your new friends, debating various options. Finally, you conclude that there are only two choices that appeal to you.

*If you believe that you must join the military struggle against the British **Mandate**, turn to page 115.*

On the other hand, if you have seen enough of war and decide to take another path, turn to page 117.

164

Y ou think back on your experiences of the last ten years. First, the **Nazis** took all your property, imprisoned you, and almost killed you. How did they manage this? It was all legal, legal, at least, in their system of "laws." Then, the British tried to keep you out of Palestine. Again, they did it with laws. Everything that they did to hinder your *aliyah* was legal, even if it was filled with anti-Semitism and bias. You are amazed at how the law can be used to help people or to make their lives miserable, and you are filled with deep resentment against those people and governments that have used laws to hurt you and others.

"That's not going to happen again, not if I can help it!" you declare. "I'm going to learn enough about laws that I shall be able to use them to help. No one will ever use the legal system of Israel to make life unbearable for another Jew."

You enroll at the **Hebrew University of Jerusalem** and study to become a lawyer. When you graduate, you become the advisor to a committee of the **Knesset** that is trying to write a new law about Israeli immigration and citizenship. Israel will not have a written constitution, but it will have a series of "organic laws," basic laws that embody fundamental values and ideas of the new country. The law that you are working on is the very first of such laws. It will be called the "**Law of Return**," and it will promise Israeli citizenship to every Jew, whether a Jew born of Jewish parents or a Jew-by-choice, who comes to settle in the new nation.

If the law is passed, but you become entangled in a controversy concerning conversion to Judaism, turn to page 10.

If you are asked to deal with a unique question of citizenship, turn to page 62.

165

There have been many days in your past when you did not have a single thing to eat. When you were running through the countryside of **Poland**, hiding from the **Nazis**, you had to scavenge for food—and sometimes you could not find anything. Then, after you were finally caught by collaborators and turned over to the **SS**, you were thrown into a forced labor camp. What they called soup was nothing but water with a little grass boiled in it, and the bread was hardly better than sawdust. Even in the **displaced persons' camp**, even when the American soldiers and the Jewish social workers tried their best, there was often very little to nourish you.

You cannot shake these memories. The pain in your stomach remains with you, and you remember how weak you felt, hardly able to raise yourself on your elbow from the wooden rack they called a bed. And you cannot forget the many people, some of them close friends of yours, who simply closed their eyes and died because they had no energy and could no longer fight the pangs of hunger.

"I promise," you think to yourself, "if for no other reason than to honor those who died, that I shall never be hungry again. I have seen and experienced the evil that comes when someone lacks food. If I do nothing else with the rest of my life, I shall make sure that neither I nor anyone else I can reach will ever suffer like that. I shall take care of my own needs, and I shall try to provide for other people."

If you decide that you can best achieve these goals by learning how to be a farmer, you should turn to page 160.

On the other hand, if you think that there may be ways you can help many people find food for themselves and their families, turn to page 11.

166

As news of the massacres at Sabra and Shatilla comes to light, you grow agitated and upset. Yes, there may be anti-Israel fighters in the refugee camps. But to kill hundreds of civilians? This is not the way Jews are supposed to act, even through their agents. And this is not the action of the Israel to which you immigrated and the Israel in which you raised your daughter.

Your Israel is a country based on Jewish religious values . . . respect for human life . . . compassion . . . justice. If Abraham could remind God [Genesis 18:25] that God had to differentiate between wicked and righteous people, between innocent and guilty, should not the same values apply to your modern society?

The government of Israel opens an inquiry and faces the facts honestly. Something went very wrong in the refugee camps. If there are Israeli military officers who played some role, that must be made known and the responsible people punished. But you cannot wait for a full investigation. Your conscience is too heavy for delay. You resign your military commission in protest. "My Israel must stand for higher values," you think. "Even by association, I will not be a party to this tragedy."

You spend the rest of your life working with an organization that helps men and women who were wounded in Israel's many wars with its neighbors. At least in this way, you can demonstrate the healing and compassionate aspect of being a Jew.

END

167

At your synagogue on **Shabbat** morning, the rabbi speaks of the biblical **prophet Joel**. "Remember what he said," the rabbi tells the congregation. "Your old men shall dream dreams, and your young men shall see visions" [Joel 3:1]. It is just such a vision that you have in mind. Solar power could change the course of history in your region of the world, a region that has been troubled by conflict, but could be led to peace by a new vision.

With the quiet agreement of the Israeli government, you send a private message to **King Hussein of Jordan**. "In the area south of the **Dead Sea**, let us make something grow. Not vegetables or trees, for the soil is too salty. No! Let us grow a field of solar collectors, shared between our two peoples, bringing a new source of energy to all the residents of our countries. Your Majesty," you continue, "I do not believe that people will fight with each other if they are linked together in a positive, constructive business project. Solar energy—and we certainly have a lot of sun—could be just such a project for peace."

Toward the end of your life, you journey south along the west shore of the **Dead Sea**. In the area of the biblical cities of **Sodom** and **Gomorrah**, you look out over the desolate valley, so contaminated with salts from the sea that nothing could ever grow there. But something has grown. Your solar collectors have sprouted from this barren wasteland, generating electricity that is now shared by **Jordan** and Israel. Joint teams of scientists work on the project. They have become friends, and never would they dream of fighting with each other. This is a vision that gives you great and abiding joy.

END

168

As one of the officers who approved the SLA raids (even though you did not expect a massacre of civilians to occur), you cannot avoid taking responsibility. You resign your commission; your military career is over. But, in your heart, you are convinced that you had made the right decision. These refugee camps were filled with enemies of Israel. The **Hezbollah** guerillas used the camps as hideouts, ducking into them after attacking Israeli settlements and concealing themselves among the civilians. Only by pursuing these terrorists right to their headquarters could Israel's security be assured. And that, you are sure, is more important than a military operation that somehow got out of control.

You settle with your family in the northern city of **Kiryat Shemona**, in the part of Israel where, you believe, you served your country with honor. You try to rebuild your life, and little by little you push the unfortunate incidents in Lebanon to the back of your mind. They are a part of your past that you would gladly forget.

But the terrorists do not forget. Not at all. One afternoon, you hear the air-raid sirens screaming. You and the other residents of this city dash toward the shelters. Then you hear the high-pitched squeal as a Katusha rocket, fired from southern **Lebanon**, crosses the border and descends toward you. It is the last thing you ever hear.

END

169

You return to the air force, now stationed at the air base at **Rosh Pina** in the **Galilee**. The Palestinian uprising in Israel, the **intifada**, has been supplied by Syrian and Lebanese forces in the **Bekaa Valley**. Arms and guerilla fighters cross the border almost every night, and the devastation they cause can be seen in the morning.

At a conference at the base, senior military officers debate what to do. Some suggest increasing patrols along the border and closing off the openings of the **Good Fence**, which has, up until now, allowed civilians to visit back and forth. "But who is a civilian today?" they ask. "Today's vegetable peddler may be tomorrow's bomb thrower."

One general takes control over the meeting. "There is only one way to deal with these people," he says. "We must attack their bases in force. Even if we have to send our army all the way to **Beirut**, we must root them out. This enemy understands only military might. We can even use our friends in the **Southern Lebanese Army** (SLA) to go into those refugee camps near **Beirut**. I am sure that is where the guerillas have their headquarters."

His opinion carries the day, and the attack is mounted. Israeli tanks and airplanes cover the infantry as the army moves quickly to the north. The SLA does its assigned task, but the results are not what anyone had anticipated. In the refugee camps of Sabra and Shatilla, a terrible massacre of civilians occurs. The SLA did more than hunt for fighting men; they killed and wounded everyone they could find.

If you are appalled by the consequences of the decision to attack, turn to page 166.

If you think what happened in the refugee camps is the unfortunate, but unavoidable result of war, turn to page 168.

170

At first, you are so angry that you can hardly breathe. How could they do this to me? How could they ruin me in this way? But then you cool down and start to think logically. Is not a little piece of rocky, dusty desert worth *shalom* between your two countries? If Israel has to give up **Taba** for peace, is that such a steep price to pay? And, after all, maybe there is a way to turn this new development into an opportunity; maybe you can see something good coming out of this change.

You arrange a meeting with the Egyptian owners of a new hotel and gambling casino that is to be located at **Taba**. "Here's my proposition," you say, as you push a sheaf of papers across the table. "You will need lots of workers to help you run this enterprise. There are not many people who live in the Egyptian **Sinai**, but there are skilled workers in **Eilat**. Think about it. Some of the new *olim* from **Russia** have spent their lives gambling for survival, gambling to get to Israel, gambling to make new lives for themselves. They would probably make excellent casino workers. I can set up a training program for them in **Eilat** and guarantee you as many trained workers as you need."

They speak to each other in Arabic and then turn back to you. "This is a very interesting proposal. We'll get back to you." You leave the meeting without an answer, but at least you have tried. You're not sure whether the Egyptians will accept your proposal or not, but you are totally sure of one thing: cooperation is worth taking a risk. No matter how this turns out, you know that you have taken a step toward peace.

END

171

This young woman, whom you have both raised to believe in working toward understanding among different groups of people, is disillusioned. During one particularly vehement argument, she pushes back from the table, stands up, and shouts: "How can you talk about peace and friendship? We live among Arabs who hate us. They would kill us if they got half a chance. Do you want to trust them? Well, I don't and I can't and I won't." With that outburst, she stalks off, and you know better than to follow her and to try to discuss the issue calmly.

Before you can find such an opportunity, she, like all other eighteen-year-olds, is called into national military service. After her initial training, she is assigned to a unit that helps teach new Jewish immigrants from **Morocco** the Hebrew language and the customs of this new country. You visit her military camp from time to time and are impressed with her maturity and teaching skill. She's really good at what she does.

Apparently, one of the new immigrants thinks so too. A dark, handsome man, he is religiously very observant. In Israel, you call such a person *dati*, which is something like **Orthodox**. Your daughter was not raised as this kind of religious Jew, but she seems attracted to it—or to him—and soon you realize that they have fallen in love. Although you are a bit uncomfortable with **Orthodox** Judaism and with Moroccan customs, you stand proudly and happily next to the *chuppah* as your daughter marries.

After several years of marriage, they invite you on a strange picnic. To find out where this trip will lead, turn to page 90.

If the path of this young couple leads into a run-down area of Tel Aviv, turn to page 91.

172

You have made a commitment to stay in the **United States** with your family, but that does not mean that, in private moments, you always feel good about your decision. There are many times when you think you really should have gone back to Israel. Yet that would have meant leaving your wife and children, and you love them very much.

You can live with your guilty feelings more easily because you have spent most of your career helping Israel—raising money, counseling and advising young people who visit there, making speeches, and teaching classes in public schools so that many students will know about your homeland. All this makes it easier to live with your decision, but you almost always feel a gnawing ambivalence.

As you reach the end of your career and prepare to retire, you visit with the rabbi of your synagogue and share your concerns with him. He leans forward and looks straight at you. "What?" he asks. "Do you think you're different from most other people? Life rarely gives us clear answers. Most of us have to live with uncertainty, doing the best we can, never being absolutely sure. But that's the way the world is. Join the crowd."

On the one hand, the rabbi's answer is true, and that makes you feel a little better. But, on the other hand, he really hasn't solved your dilemma. Your satisfaction about living in **America** and your guilt about not being in Israel—both are true. Then, you laugh to yourself. "But that's the way the world is. Join the crowd."

END

173

Michael Gorbachev, the leader of the **Soviet Union**, has adopted a new policy, *perestroika.* He means to create a society that is more democratic and open, in which people have more rights. One of the rights he offers is the chance for Jews to leave this country, which has, throughout its history, not been very hospitable to Jews.

As some of these new Americans arrive in your community, you get to know them and hear the stories of how they left their homes. Even with *perestroika,* it was very difficult, and they had to leave behind family and friends and many of their possessions. You help them make a new place for themselves in this, their adopted homeland.

An idea occurs to you: if you could get into **Russia** and help them before they left, it would be easier for them to resettle in a new land. And you might be able to convince more of them to move to Israel. You secure a job with the **Jewish Agency for Israel** and are assigned to the southern Russian city of **Rostov**, a city with a million Russians and about ten thousand Jews. There, you can teach Hebrew to those who plan to leave, help them understand what their new lives might be like, and give them confidence that this is the right move for them—and, especially, for their children's future.

As you continue your work in **Rostov**, something happens that causes you to question whether you ought to stay there.

To find out what this new development is, turn to page 58.

174

Everyone on the street is buzzing with news. No one knows exactly what has happened, but it is clearly something important. You rush home and turn on the television set. The news announcer from Kol Yisrael, the official Israeli television station, looks directly into the camera with a somber face. "I have to inform you that an **El Al** plane has been hijacked by Arab terrorists. They have landed in **Uganda**; the passengers are being held hostage at the airport in **Entebbe**. We shall give you more details as soon as they are available."

Israel's air force and commando units mobilize immediately. A rescue mission must be organized. No one will permit Israelis to be held captive in this way. With great secrecy, planes fly down the **Red Sea**, turn inland over **Kenya** (their friendly government has given permission for the raid to fly over their territory), and then swoop over the capital city of **Kampala** to the airport. The arrival of Israel's commando troops is a total surprise. The hostages are rescued with few injuries; only one soldier, the commander of the mission, **Yonatan Netanyahu**, dies of a gunshot wound. A hero has died. But overall, a great victory has happened there. Terrorists must realize that there is no place they can hide in safety.

You are convinced even more that you were right; the Arabs cannot be trusted. Israel's Jewish population must be increased as rapidly as possible by immigration. You commit yourself to the **mitzvah** of *pidyon sh'vuyim*, rescuing Jews who are captive anywhere in the world.

If this leads you to help young Russian **olim** *make a new life in Israel, turn to page 178.*

If you adopt a new family of Russian immigrants, turn to page 179.

175

Around the bend, you come upon a squarish building with a tall tower, a minaret. Even from a distance, you can see that this is where the problem occurred, for there is a commotion of people running back and forth, screaming, crying. Obviously, something terrible has happened. "Be careful, men! This looks like a dangerous situation. Don't do anything to make it worse," you say.

As a leader, you have a special responsibility. You walk ahead of your troops and look for someone from the Arab community who seems to be in charge. A tall, straight, distinguished man stands out, so you approach him. "What has happened here?" you ask. "What has happened! One of your crazy settlers burst into the **mosque** and started shooting. Many people are dead. Many others are wounded. How could anyone do this? He must have been insane. And he is dead, too. Either he shot himself or one of us did. In either case, it's a punishment that comes from *Allah*. Good riddance!"

You know the dead man. You have seen him in the settlements. But how, you wonder, could anyone who claimed to be a religious **Orthodox** Jew do something like this? "This is not religious," you say to your men. "Judaism can never say that this kind of massacre is permitted. I don't understand how this could occur."

If you go to the settlement to try to make sense out of this act, turn to page 180.

If you realize that the bloodshed will continue until another way is found, turn to page 89.

176

Your men look around nervously. Where did the gunfire come from? Are they in danger? Before they have a chance to reach any conclusions, two young men race down the road toward you. "Quick! Hurry! Get an ambulance! They have shot Yaron."

A Palestinian sniper, hiding on a rooftop in nearby **Hebron**, took aim at this young settler as he walked through the streets of **Kiryat Arba**. The rifle bullet pierced his chest, but as the paramedics lift the stretcher into the ambulance and drive away, he is still alive. As fast as possible, they drive north toward the **Hadassah Hospital** in **Jerusalem**. There, the very best doctors in Israel examine him. "He is going to die," they conclude. "But his kidneys are healthy. We could save two lives if we would be permitted to take them after he dies and transplant them into two other people."

This is an operation that has not been performed in this hospital before now. In fact, the doctors do not even know whether they will be permitted to do it. One of them, a doctor who is an **Orthodox** Jew, says, "I don't think we can do the operation unless we get permission from the rabbinical council. And I don't know how they will rule, or even if they can act fast enough so that we can still use these organs."

To find out what the rabbinical authorities say, turn to page 97.

177

The young people in *tzofim* go on long fitness hikes through the hills of the **Golan**. They learn how to survive by gathering fruit that grows wild on vines and collecting water from cactus plants. Over time, they study first aid and how to predict the weather. Although they hardly knew each other before joining the group, now they would trust each other with their lives.

Like almost all Israeli young people, they accept the obligation of military service after high school. Your friend the **madrich** is very proud of them. They are the best of Israel's youth. Some of them even become officers in the army, and you are glad to salute them when they come home in their uniforms.

One day, an army officer he does not know enters the **madrich's** office. The officer has a serious look on his face and, even without an invitation, takes a chair. "I have news you don't want to hear," he says. "Four of the young people you trained in *tzofim* were on patrol in southern **Lebanon**. I am sorry to tell you that all of them were killed."

He is devastated and comes to speak with you. These young people, barely in their twenties, were like his own children. Hot tears stream down his face, and he buries his head in his hands, hoping to block out this horrible report. But there is no avoiding it. Nor is it possible to deny that his training helped put them in harm's way. "It's not right," he says to you, "that all the time we spent together should lead to this fate. It's just not fair."

Yet Israeli young people will always have to be soldiers. Isn't it better that they be well prepared? You remind him that that's the gift he offers them through the *tzofim*. With heavy heart, he decides he has no alternative but to continue his work. You wish things were easier. But you are proud of this caring, dedicated **madrich**.

END

178

A new suburb of **Jerusalem, Mevasseret Zion**, lies just to the west of Israel's capital city. Many of the residents of this new area are *olim* who are recently arrived from various parts of the **Soviet Union**. These Russian, Ukrainian, and Byelorussian Jews are anxious to create new lives for themselves in the Jewish state, and they appreciate the help and guidance that you are able to give them. The fact that you once had to do the same thing for yourself makes what you say very believable to them.

With the help of some of these young men and women, you build a new school building to house programs for the very youngest children. The preschool and kindergarten will be run by the **Israel Movement for Progressive Judaism**, which is what **Reform Judaism** is called in Israel. Their schools in Israel are very popular, especially with immigrant Russian Jews, who have not had much experience with or education about the Jewish religion. Soon, the school is filled with children laughing, playing, and learning.

But one night you are awakened by yells from the direction of the school building. As you run down the street, you stop in horror. Flames shoot high out of the roof of the structure; it is a total loss. Who could have done such a thing? An ultra-**Orthodox** group that has a fanatic dislike for liberal Judaism is blamed, but no one can prove anything. You know for sure that you must rebuild the school and continue helping these new citizens of Israel in making their difficult journey from **Russia** something very positive.

As you watch the first graduation of the kindergarten in **Mevasseret Zion**, you are sure that this is the highest achievement of your life. You know that the ideals you believe in will be carried on into the next generation.

END

179

As the airplane taxis up to the airport steps, you can hardly contain your excitement. When you lived in the city of **Brest** in **Byelorussia**, you had met a young Jewish family. Now you find it hard to believe that they have made *aliyah* with their two children and that they are really on this plane. Then the door opens, and you wave your blue and white flag as your friends descend into their brand-new life.

That evening, over a cup of tea, you talk with them about their future. In **Brest**, the father was a violinist. He played with the symphony and taught private students. But here, there are many violinists and only a few jobs. All of you realize that he must find another kind of work. What could he do? It turns out that he likes to repair things, and soon he has a small shop where people bring household objects to be fixed. It's not exactly the work he used to do in **Brest**, and maybe it will not be the work he will end up doing here, but he has to start somewhere.

His son, however, is very upset. At sixteen, he is embarrassed that his father, once a leading musician in **Russia**, now must repair clocks and lamps and other household items. This is hard work, and it doesn't pay very well. With youthful impatience, he is convinced that there must be a quicker, easier way to get rich in Israel.

If he takes a path that both you and his parents disapprove of, turn to page 86.

If your own son decides to get involved, turn to page 68.

180

The settlement perches on top of a low hill. It is little more than a collection of prefabricated homes and some barbed wire fences around its property, hardly the dream of a "land flowing with milk and honey" that you read about in the Bible. The people who have come to live here, however, are totally committed to their cause. "We were promised this entire land by God in the Bible. We are doing nothing more than claiming what is rightfully ours. The Arabs have no right to live here. They must leave, and if they will not, then we shall be at war and we shall drive them away. They would kill us if they could, so we must defend ourselves. If we have to kill them first, so be it."

That the Arabs have also lived in this region since biblical times doesn't move these zealots of the **Gush Emunim**. That the Bible tells you that murder is wrong, that God forbids it—this, too, they reject. "This is a holy war," they say, "a war for the land that we were promised by God. In such a war, anything is permitted."

As you leave their little home, you shake your head in disbelief. These do not seem to be evil people. They sincerely believe that they are doing what God wants them to do. But their acts are evil, this much you know for sure. Killing other people can never be justified as a way to settle an argument. There must be another way, though you do not see it right now. You walk down the road, thinking about a better path to peace, when you hear the crack of a distant rifle shot. The thudding impact of the bullet spins you around, and you fall to the ground. Blood streams from your chest. You start to say the *Sh'ma*. It is the . . .

END

181

Ever since you saw **Hitler** demand one hundred percent agreement in **Germany**, you have been against the requirement of total conformity. "Adults have the right to make choices," you say. "There must be many paths to a praiseworthy goal, even many ways to be a godly person and a good Jew. Who says a **Reform** or Conservative conversion is less Jewish than an **Orthodox** one? Except **Orthodox** rabbis who, you should pardon my frankness, may be more interested in keeping their power than doing what's good for the Jewish people."

Delegations of liberal Jews from the **Diaspora** flood into Israel to protest the conversion proposal. "If this passes," they announce, "the millions of Jews who live outside the Land of Israel will feel cut off from Israel. This one act will have a devastating result on both their feelings for this special nation and for their willingness to support it with their *tzedakah* and with their political efforts. We cannot let this happen."

You meet with many of these groups and come to believe that they are right. If the **Knesset** passes this change in the **Law of Return**, there will be a dangerous splitting of the Jewish people. The anger that will be kindled among Jews in other countries is simply not worth making this change, even though the **Orthodox** rabbis very much want it. You have to stop their campaign.

*If you embark on a speaking tour in the **United States**, turn to page 38.*

If you realize that the long-range solution to this issue is to build up a liberal Jewish movement in Israel, turn to page 39.

182

As far to the south as you can go in Israel, there is a dusty little town named **Eilat**. Just to its east is the Jordanian town of **Aqaba**; farther to the east, you can see the reddish hills of **Saudi Arabia**, while to the west is the Egyptian **Sinai Peninsula**. Four countries form the coastline of the **Gulf of Aqaba**, a body of warm, blue-green water with many kinds of colorful fish swimming through the coral reefs that grow just beneath the surface of the water.

"If you look at **Eilat** right now, you won't be impressed," says the man you are standing with on the beach. "But have a little vision. Try to imagine what it might be like in ten years, with tourist hotels lining a wide avenue along the shore, palm trees swaying in the gentle breeze, **falafel** vendors hawking their wares from little pushcarts, and boats taking tourists out to the reefs so that they can dive into the clear water and see one of nature's most beautiful sights. Have a little vision, my friend. You could be a big part of this economic development at the southern tip of our country."

With your eyes now opened to new possibilities, you visualize what your friend has been telling you. He's right. There are huge opportunities in this little village. It's small now, but it could be an immense new center for Israel's tourist industry in the future. You've got to have a share in this expansion.

If you love the sea and want to do something connected with it, turn to page 161.

If, however, you want to be more practical and develop a project that will be directly useful to the tourists, turn to page 144.

183

The sleek passenger liner sits in the harbor of **Ashdod**, while you and the other craftspeople paint the murals for its walls and finish furnishing it for its first trans-Atlantic journey. The inside of the ship smells of paint, so you eat your lunch sitting on the deck and enjoying the sun and the sea breeze.

An unusual sound disturbs you. You look around, then up. A blue and white airplane floats gently in the air, gliding in from the sea, turning left toward the airport outside **Tel Aviv**. It is one of the planes from **El Al**, Israel's new international airline. Against the blue sky, it is a beautiful sight.

You love painting the murals of the *Shalom*. You can depict the most wonderful events in the Jewish past for all the passengers to enjoy. This is a great job! Just the kind of work you would have created for yourself if you could have had all the choices in the world.

But you also realize that the ship will be very slow. It will take nearly two weeks to sail from **New York** to **Tel Aviv**. On **El Al**, the same journey will take less than one day. Traveling by ship may be luxurious and fun, but it will not be fast enough for your daughter and her generation. She will need something else for her life.

If your daughter grows up and wants to join the air force, turn to page 29.

If she realizes that her future as a pilot will be limited, but is determined to have something to do with aviation, turn to page 31.

184

Maybe there was something your daughter's young man missed. Maybe he only heard part of what the rabbis were telling him. After all, it's an old Jewish practice to try to discourage a potential convert, just to be sure that they are really convinced of what they want to do.

But you haven't been in touch with much about **Orthodox** Judaism since you were a **bar mitzvah** in prewar **Poland**. Maybe it's time you learned a little more about this form of Judaism. To follow through on this idea, you enroll in classes at the Yeshivat HaKotel, a school in **Jerusalem**'s **Old City** that specializes in teaching *baalei t'shuvah*. As you study there, you understand their belief that this is the true force of Judaism, one that is faithful to the words of the Torah and to the interpretations of those words that have come down through the ages.

You cannot accept this idea yourself, but meanwhile your son is gradually becoming more and more **Orthodox**. He moves into **Meah Shearim**, the section of the city where the most orthodox of all **Orthodox** Jews live. At an angry confrontation in your house, you and your wife challenge him: "What about us? Are you so self-centered that you will do only what you want and leave us behind—or force us to accept your ways?"

"That's about it," he replies. "I have learned what God wants me to do. If you cannot accept that path, I am sorry, but I must do what I must do. I am satisfied with my decision. You will make your own life; I've made mine. And it is right!"

END

185

You find a new home for yourself, in the seaside city of **Netanya**, where you begin to teach the new immigrants about Israel. But it is also time for you to settle down. Soon, you find a wonderful woman, a social worker among these same refugees. Your shared passion for helping these desperate immigrants draws you together, and you marry. Within a year, your daughter is born, and you rejoice at the blessings of your new life.

As your daughter grows, she, too, believes that the most important **mitzvot** she can perform are saving Jews who are persecuted elsewhere in the world and welcoming these strangers into the Land of Israel. As your daughter matures into a young woman in her own right, you gain great satisfaction knowing that the work to which you and your wife dedicated your lives will continue.

If your daughter decides to strike out on her own, turn to page 47.

If you decide that you will all continue the resettlement work together, turn to page 48.

186

Farther north, just to the west of **Lake Hula**, you find such a place. The **kibbutz** there is called **Mishmar Hayarden**, "Lookout Post Over the Jordan Valley." It was one of the very first settlements created by the *yishuv*, back in the 1880s. More recently, it earned its name when it was on the front lines of the battle with the Syrian army during the **War of Independence**, and only a few months ago were Israeli soldiers able to wrest it from the control of the occupying Arab military forces.

The area around this settlement—well, you would hardly wish it on your worst enemy. It is swampy. Marshes are filled with water, and disease-causing insects abound. Living at **Mishmar Hayarden** would test anyone's ideals, even without the occasional artillery shell that sails in from the Syrian guns on the **Golan Heights**. Life here will certainly not be easy. But you really want to see if you can handle a difficult challenge and make a real contribution to building up the land.

You move to **Mishmar Hayarden** and immediately decide that your task will be to help drain the marshland and create ponds where the **kibbutz** can raise fish. And just a year later, as you and your family relax over a **Shabbat** meal of tender fish, you understand that your life has been fulfilled. You have met the challenge and made a difference in this new land. What else could anyone really ask for?

END

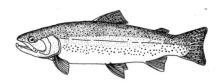

187

The music director of the Israel Philharmonic seeks your granddaughter out. "I understand that you love the music of the Jewish past, but that you also understand classical and modern concert music. Is that right?" "Yes, sir, it is."

"Good! Then, you might be interested in a job with our orchestra. Not playing, to be sure, but in the music library. We need someone who understands and appreciates all different kinds of music, who can help me sort through the hundreds of scores that might be chosen for a program so that I can find just the right combination of pieces."

She takes the job. Sometimes, she travels with the Philharmonic as they play concerts throughout the world. But, as she tells you in a special, quiet moment, her favorite place to be with the orchestra is in the Roman amphitheater in **Caesarea**. "As I look out over the ancient stones toward the old Roman port and the **Mediterranean** beyond it, I can visualize all the musicians of our past. They are now part of me, and I am part of them. We play the music of our people together, at least in my mind, and I love it. What a great place to be! What a great job to have! I am truly blessed."

And if she is so happy, then you, her grandfather, feel enormous joy. If you have done nothing else with your life, to have helped raise such a wonderful granddaughter makes your entire life worthwhile.

END

GLOSSARY

abba • Hebrew, "father."

Abraham and Sarah • The first of the great Patriarchs (fathers) and Matriarchs (mothers) of the Jewish people. Their stories are told in Genesis 12–25.

African Hebrew Israelites • African–Americans who follow the Jewish religion and claim direct descent from biblical personalities.

Al-Aqsa Mosque • A very important **Moslem** place of worship located on the ancient **Temple Mount** in **Jerusalem**. During times of political unrest in the area, it has been closed off to Jewish tourists.

Albright, William (1891–1971) • American biblical archaeologist who led the **American School of Oriental Research** in **Jerusalem**.

alef-bet • Hebrew, "alphabet."

aliyah • Hebrew, "going up"—going up to the pulpit to say the blessings over the Torah during services or, here, going up/immigrating to Israel.

Allah • Arabic, "God."

American School of Oriental Research (ASOR) • Center of biblical archaeological studies located in the eastern sector of **Jerusalem**. During Jordanian occupation before 1967, ASOR was not accessible to Jews.

Amos • Biblical prophet who lived about 750 B.C.E. in and around **Jerusalem**.

Am Yisrael chai • Hebrew, "the people of Israel lives."

Arab Legion • An elite unit of the Jordanian army.

Arafat, Yasir • Leader of the **Palestine Liberation Organization**, an organization based in Syria after 1956 that fought for rights of Palestinian

Arabs, especially those who had fled Israel in 1947–1949. After 1967, the PLO led terror attacks on Israelis both in and outside of Israel.

Ashtarte • Female goddess/idol of Canaanite religion in biblical times.

Auschwitz • Extermination camp near **Cracow (Poland)** operated by Germans during World War II. It is estimated that 2 million Jews were murdered at Auschwitz.

baal t'shuvah • Hebrew, "a Jew who was not observant but who has now changed and has become an **Orthodox** Jew."

Babylonian Talmud • A multivolume set of commentaries on the **Mishnah** that was completed about 600 C.E. and that remains today the primary source of Jewish law and thought.

Baha'i • Religion founded in Iran about 1850 C.E. Driven out of that country in 1867, its followers established a headquarters in **Haifa**, Israel. Baha'is believe in the unity of all people and religions.

bar mitzvah • Ceremony during which a thirteen-year-old boy is recognized as an adult in the Jewish religion.

baruch haba • Hebrew, "blessed be he who comes" or "welcome."

Bedouins • Nomadic Arabs who live in the desert regions of Israel. Their lifestyle is very similar to that of shepherds in biblical times.

Begin, Menachem (b. Poland, 1913; d. Israel, 1993) • Entered Palestine in 1942 and fought for Israel's independence. Held many political posts, including that of prime minister.

Ben-Gurion, David (b. Russian Poland, 1886; d. Israel, 1973) • Settled in Palestine in 1906 and is recognized as one of the primary founders of the Jewish state. He served as prime minister and defense minister from 1948–1953 and 1956–1963.

Ben-Gurion University of the Negev • A major center of academic studies located in **Beersheba** and named after **David Ben-Gurion**.

Ben Zakkai, Yochanan • Rabbi who lived during the Roman destruction of **Jerusalem** (68–70 C.E.) and who helped Judaism survive after that disaster.

Bezalel • Expert artist who led workers in the construction of the biblical Tabernacle (see: Exodus 31, 36–39).

Biran, Avraham (1909–present) • Israeli archaeologist and diplomat, best known for his excavation of Tel Dan.

b'rachah • Hebrew, "blessing."

Chabad • **Chasidic** Jewish group, sometimes known as **Lubavitch.** The three Hebrew letters that form the basis of the word stand for "wisdom," "knowledge," and "understanding."

challah • Bread used during Friday evening meal over which a blessing is said to thank God for everything that nourishes and sustains us.

Chanukah dreidel • A small top used to play a game during Chanukah. In the **Diaspora**, its sides are marked with four Hebrew letters that stand for the phrase "a great miracle happened there." In Israel, the last word is changed to "here."

Chasidim • **Chasidic** or Ultra-**Orthodox** Jews who belong to various sects led by **rebbes.**

chazan • Hebrew, "cantor" or leader of religious services, especially their musical parts.

cheder • Hebrew, "room." Refers to traditional Jewish elementary school.

chuppah • Canopy under which a Jewish wedding takes place.

Communist Party • Political party based on the ideas of Karl Marx that controlled the former **Soviet Union** from 1917 until 1991. Stills exists in **Russia** and many other countries, but without its former power or influence.

dati • Hebrew, "religious" or "law abiding." Usually refers to **Orthodox** Jews.

daven • Yiddish, "to pray" usually in a swaying fashion.

Diaspora • From Greek, "scattering" or "dispersion." Refers to Jews who live in many places outside the Land of Israel.

displaced persons' camp • A place, often in or near **Germany**, where people who had been removed from their homes during World War II and who had often been imprisoned in concentration camps could be housed until they could return home or find a new place to live.

Dizengoff Street • Main street in downtown **Tel Aviv**.

Dome of the Rock • **Moslem** shrine on the top of the **Temple Mount** in **Jerusalem**, marking the place from which Mohammed rose up to heaven. The site is closed to Jewish visitors at times of political unrest in the region.

Don Avia • The airline of the Don region of southern **Russia**.

Eban, Abba (b. South Africa, 1915–present) • Israeli statesman, diplomat, and author.

El Al • Israel's national airline.

Elijah • Biblical prophet (I Kings 17–19, II Kings 1–2, and Malachi 4) most especially known in Jewish tradition as the messenger who will announce publicly the coming of the Messiah or Messianic age.

Eretz Yisrael • Hebrew, "the Land of Israel."

Exodus • The second book of the Torah, which tells the story of the flight of the Israelites from Egyptian slavery. In 1947, a ship on which 4,500 European Jews attempted to enter Palestine illegally after World War II. Captured by the British navy, they were taken back to **displaced persons' camps** in **Germany**, but most eventually entered Israel after independence.

falafel • A small, deep-fried ball of ground-up chickpeas and spices eaten in a **pita** bread with lettuce, tomato, and dressing.

Fatah • **Yasir Arafat**'s organization within the **Palestine Liberation Organization** that rejected the existence of Israel as a Jewish state and sought by any means, including terrorist attacks, to destroy the state.

Federation • The central fund-raising and planning agency of a Jewish community. In French-speaking countries, it is called "Consistoire," and in German-speaking areas, "Gemeinde."

Frank, Anne (b. Holland, 1929; d. Bergen Belsen, 1945) • Dutch girl who hid during most of World War II with her family in an attic in **Amsterdam**. Captured by the Nazis, she died in **Bergen-Belsen** concentration camp.

freilach • Yiddish, "joyous." A particularly happy kind of music played by a **klezmer** band.

Galitzianer • A person who comes from Galitzia (Galicia), an area today that would include parts of southern **Poland**, Slovakia, **Hungary**, and **Belarus**.

Gestapo • The **Nazi** secret police during World War II.

Glueck, Nelson (b. 1900; d. 1971, both in Cincinnati, Ohio) • American rabbi and archaeologist who explored Israel's **Negev** region; president of the **Hebrew Union College–Jewish Institute of Religion** from 1948–1971.

Good Fence • The dividing line between northern Israel and **Lebanon**. Known by this title because, for a long time, relations between the people on both sides were rather friendly.

Gorbachev, Michael (1931–present) • Premier of the **Soviet Union** until its breakup in 1991.

Greater Israel • A theory, advanced by some groups in Israel and their allies elsewhere, that Jews have a right to the maximum territory described as Israel in the Bible. This territory would be considerably larger than the present State of Israel.

Green Line • Boundary between Israeli and Jordanian parts of Palestine (especially **Jerusalem**) before 1967. After the Six-Day War, Israel took possession of both sides of the line.

Guide for the Perplexed • Book written by **Moses Maimonides** that sought to merge Jewish religious wisdom and Greek philosophical ideas.

Gush Emunim • Modern group of **Orthodox** Jews in Israel who believe in the idea of **Greater Israel** and who try to establish settlements to expand the Jewish presence into new areas.

Hadassah Hospital • Major medical institution in Jerusalem, founded and supported by the Women's International Zionist Organization (Hadassah in the **United States**).

haftarah • A selection from the biblical prophets that is read in the synagogue during Shabbat morning services.

Haganah • The Jewish self-defense organization in pre-independence Palestine. Founded in 1920, it became the core of Israel's army in 1948.

Hakotel • Hebrew, "the Wall." Refers to a high wall on the west side of the **Temple Mount** in **Jerusalem** that is a sacred place for Jews.

halachah • Hebrew, "law." Refers to Jewish religious law embodied in the **Babylonian Talmud** and commentaries on it.

Hammer, Gottlieb (1911–1993) • American-Jewish communal executive who was a key liaison with the *yishuv* and Israel as the nation developed. His last post was as head of the United Israel Appeal, where he raised money through donations and bank loans that Israel required for critical human services.

HaMotzi • Hebrew, "who brings forth." Refers to the blessing said before eating bread or other similar foods to thank God for that which keeps us alive.

Har El • Hebrew, "mountain of God." A **Reform** Jewish congregation in **Jerusalem**.

"Hatikvah" • Hebrew, "The Hope." Israel's national anthem based on a poem composed by Naftali Herz Imber in 1878.

Hebrew Union College–Jewish Institute of Religion (HUC-JIR) • Seminary and graduate school of **Reform Judaism**. HUC was founded by Isaac Mayer Wise in 1875; JIR was established by Stephen S. Wise in 1922. They merged in 1948 and now have campuses in Cincinnati, New York, Los Angeles, and Jerusalem.

Hebrew University of Jerusalem • Major university in Israel. Founded in **Jerusalem** in 1918.

Herzl, Theodor (1860–1904) • Austrian journalist who founded the modern Zionist movement and who worked tirelessly to establish a Jewish state in Palestine.

Hezbollah • Anti-Israel guerrilla group based in southern **Lebanon** and western **Syria**.

High Holy Days • Rosh HaShanah (the Jewish New Year) and Yom Kippur (the Day of Atonement); a ten-day period of spiritual self-examination and renewal that occurs in the fall.

Hitler, Adolf (1889–1945) • Founder of the National Socialist **(Nazi)** Party and leader of **Germany**'s Third Reich from 1933–1945, during which period 6 million Jews and countless others were murdered.

ima • Hebrew, "mother."

intifada • Uprising of Palestinian and Israeli Arabs to oppose Israel and various Israeli policies; often marked by street riots and violence.

Irgun Tz'va-i L'umi • Jewish underground armed organization founded in 1931, originally to protect Jewish settlers from Arab attacks. After 1939, fought against British troops occupying Palestine. Disbanded in 1948, but the Cherut political party carries on some of its ideas. Most famous member was **Menachem Begin**.

Islam • Major world religion founded by Mohammed about 630 C.E.

Isaiah • Name of two biblical **prophet**s, the first of whose writings date from 722–701 B.C.E. and the second of whom is dated after 538 B.C.E.

Israel Movement for Progressive Judaism • The liberal or **Reform** Jewish movement in modern Israel.

Jacob and Esau • The twin sons of Isaac and Rebekah. Their stories can be found in Genesis 27–36.

Jeremiah • Biblical **prophet** whose writings began about 610 B.C.E. and continued past 587 B.C.E., when most of the Jews of Canaan were taken into exile in Babylonia.

Jewish Agency for Israel • Executive body of the World Zionist Organization responsible for many functions in Palestine and early Israel, such as immigrant absorption, agricultural settlement, education in the **Diaspora**, youth activities, etc. Largely taken over by the Israeli government today.

Jewish Anti-Fascist Committee • Group of Soviet Jewish intellectuals organized in 1941 to rally support for **Russia** in World War II. Disbanded in 1948, its members were arrested and executed in 1952 on orders of **Josef Stalin**.

Jewish Brigade • British army unit during World War II. Fought in North Africa and Italy, then helped smuggle Jews from **displaced persons' camps** into Palestine. Disbanded in 1946.

Jewish National Fund (JNF) • Created in 1901 to purchase land and develop it in Palestine. By 1948, JNF owned over half of all land in the new State of Israel. Continues to improve Israel's land, especially by planting forests.

Joel • Biblical **prophet** of unknown date.

Joint Distribution Committee (American Jewish JDC) • Created in 1914 to deal with human service needs during World War I, it continues to provide relief and rescue activities for Jews throughout the world.

Kabbalah • Jewish mystical teachings based on the *Zohar*, a book written by Moses de Leon in about 1245 C.E. in southern France.

Kaddish • A prayer praising God; often used when people are mourning or remembering someone who has died.

Kahane, Meir (1932–1990) • U.S.-born rabbi who moved to Israel and led a political-religious movement that espoused **Greater Israel** and the expulsion of Arab residents.

kibbutz (plural: kibbutzim) • Community based on the ideal of social equality, collective property, production, and consumption. A **kibbutznik** is a resident of a **kibbutz**.

Kiddush • Prayer over wine that praises God for creation (the good things we can enjoy) and the **Exodus** from **Egypt** (our freedom).

King Abdullah of Jordan • Became king under the British in 1946 when the region was called Transjordan and then king of the Hashemite kingdom of **Jordan** in 1950. He actively negotiated with Israel to find a peaceful solution to the Palestinian conflict, but this position placed him in strong conflict with the other Arab countries, and he was assassinated in **Jerusalem** by an Arab nationalist in 1951.

King Hussein of Jordan • Succeeded the assassinated **King Abdullah** (his father) in 1951 and remained king until his death in 1999.

King Solomon (ca. 950–900 B.C.E.) • Biblical king of Israel who built the Temple in **Jerusalem** and expanded the borders of the Jewish state to their maximum extent.

klezmer • Eastern European style of Jewish music that is usually happy and upbeat.

Knesset • Israel's parliament.

Kollek, Teddy (1911–present) • Long-time mayor of **Jerusalem** who worked to have better relations with Israeli Arabs.

kol Yisrael • Hebrew, "all of Israel." Refers to the Jewish people as a collective whole.

Kremlin • The fortress in the center of **Moscow** where the Russian government has its headquarters.

Lag BaOmer • Thirty-third day of the counting of the barley harvest. The one day between Passover and Shavuot on which traditional Jews may marry.

Ladino • A language combining Hebrew and Spanish that was spoken widely in Jewish communities around the **Mediterranean**.

Law of Return • The first so-called "organic law" passed by the **Knesset** in 1948. It guarantees Israeli citizenship to any Jew who makes *aliyah*.

Lipman, Eugene (1919–1993) • **Reform** Jewish rabbi and social activist who served as chaplain in the U.S. army during and immediately after World War II. Active in rescuing and resettling survivors of the *Shoah*.

Litvak • Yiddish, a Jew from Lithuania.

Lubavitch Chasid • Group of ultra-**Orthodox** Jews founded by Schneur Zalman of Lyady in **Poland** about 1800. Also known as **Chabad**.

Lubyanka • Prison in Moscow where the secret police interrogated and tortured political opponents of the country's **Communist** rulers.

Maccabee(s) • Name applied to the descendants of Mattathias the Hasmonean who revolted against **Syria** in 168 B.C.E. and restored the Temple in **Jerusalem** to Jewish worship in 165 B.C.E. Also two books in the nonbiblical collection called Apocrypha.

madrich • Leader, especially of a youth group or scouting troop.

Maimonides, Moses (Rambam) (1135–1204) • Outstanding rabbi, philosopher, and physician. Born in Spain, but fled persecution to **Egypt**, where he died.

Mandate • Authority given by the League of Nations in 1920 to Great Britain, permitting that country to govern Palestine. Terminated on May 14, 1948, when Israel became independent.

Marcus, David (1902–1948) • U.S. army officer who joined Israeli troops in the **War of Independence**. Accidentally killed by his own soldiers.

Meir, Golda (1898–1978) • Born in **Russia**, raised in the **United States**, she made *aliyah* in 1921 and became an influential leader in government and labor unions. First Israeli diplomat to be sent to Russia and prime minister of Israel from 1969–1974.

menschlichkeit • Yiddish, "human decency, politeness, and respect for other people."

Mesopotamia • The region of today's **Iraq** between the Tigris and Euphrates Rivers.

M'gillah • Hebrew, "scroll." Refers to the biblical Book of Esther.

midrash (plural: midrashim) • Usually nonlegal commentaries on the Bible that contain ethical and moral stories and guidance.

Mishnah • Book of basic Jewish laws compiled by Rabbi Y'hudah HaNasi about 200 C.E. in the **Galilee**.

mitzvah (plural: mitzvot) • Hebrew, "divine commandment." The Torah contains 613 mitzvot. Sometimes used to mean "good deed."

Moses • Biblical hero who led the Israelites from Egyptian slavery to freedom and received the Torah from God at Mount Sinai.

moshav • Agricultural settlement in Israel in which most decisions are made collectively but where property may be held privately.

Moshiach • Hebrew and Yiddish, "Messiah."

Moslem • Someone who follows the religion of Islam.

mosque • Islamic place of meeting and prayer.

Nabatean • Semitic people who lived in southern **Jordan** about 250 B.C.E.–500 C.E.

Nazi • Abbreviation for "National Socialist." Follower of **Adolf Hitler**.

Netanyahu, Yonatan (Yoni) (1946–1976) • Israeli army officer killed during raid in Entebbe (**Uganda**) to free Israeli hostages taken prisoner during a "skyjacking."

New World • Refers to lands west of the Atlantic Ocean (**Canada, United States**, Central and **South America**).

olim • Hebrew, "immigrants to Israel."

Operation Magic Carpet • Israeli airlift in 1948–1950 of about 50,000 Jews from **Yemen** and **Aden** to Israel.

Orthodox • Jews who believe that the Torah came directly from God to Moses and that, therefore, they must follow the **mitzvot** as precisely as possible.

Palestine Liberation Organization (PLO) • Organization dedicated to gaining rights for Arabs either living in Israel or who were displaced during 1948 **War of Independence**. See also **Arafat**.

Palmach • From 1941–1948, a military unit of the **Haganah**.

Peres, Shimon (1923–present) • Israeli politician who made *aliyah* from **Belarus** in 1934 and has held many significant posts in Israel's government.

perestroika • Plan by **Gorbachev** to increase freedom and economic growth in the **Soviet Union**.

Pesach • Hebrew, "Passover." The festival that commemorates the Israelites' freedom from Egyptian slavery.

Philistines • Biblical people who lived on the seacoast between Israel and **Egypt**.

pidyon sh'vuyim • Hebrew, "ransoming captives (or prisoners)."

pikuach nefesh • Hebrew, "saving a life."

pita • A flat bread with a pocket inside. See **falafel**.

pogrom • Russian, "thunderclap." A riot against Jews either sponsored or permitted by the tzarist government.

prophet • Biblical leader who analyzed the behavior of the Israelites in comparison to the expectations of the Torah and described the consequences of that behavior to the people.

Rabbanut • Chief council of Orthodox Rabbis in Israel.

Rabin, Yitzchak (1922–1995) • Israeli political leader and prime minister. Assassinated by right-wing Israeli zealot who feared he might negotiate too generously with the Arabs.

rebbe • Yiddish, "leader of a **Chasidic** group."

Reform Judaism • Style of Judaism that emerged about 1800 in **Germany** and spread extensively, especially in North America. Holds that the Torah and **halachah** are not binding, but that they can be modified in accordance with the needs of modern times.

Reform Synagogue of Great Britain • Organization of liberal Jewish congregations in Great Britain.

rosh yeshivah • Hebrew, "head of an academy of higher Jewish studies."

saba • Hebrew, "grandfather."

sabra • Hebrew, "cactus" or cactus pear, the fruit of the cactus. Refers to native-born Israelis, as many believe Israelis to be prickly on the outside, sweet on the inside, not unlike the fruit.

Sadat, Anwar (1918–1981) • President of **Egypt** who flew to Israel in 1977 to discuss a possible peace treaty. Assassinated by **Moslem** extremists who did not want any relationship with the Jewish state.

Second Temple • After the Jews returned from Babylonian exile in 538 B.C.E., they rebuilt the destroyed First Temple.

Sephardic Jew • A descendant of Jews expelled from Spain in 1492, usually living around the **Mediterranean** or in the Middle East.

Shavuot • Feast of Weeks, which occurs fifty days after Passover. Celebrates both the first harvest and the revelation of the Torah on Mount Sinai. See also **Lag BaOmer**.

Shabbat *(Shabbes)* • Hebrew (Yiddish), "Sabbath."

shalom • Hebrew, "peace," and a general word of greeting.

shanda • Yiddish, "disgrace."

Shin Bet • Israeli secret service and domestic intelligence division.

Shoah • Hebrew, "great fire"; the Holocaust.

shtetl • (**plural:** *shtetlach*) Small Eastern European town before World War II with a large percentage of Jewish residents.

shuk • Hebrew, "marketplace."

shul • Yiddish, "synagogue."

siddur • Hebrew, "prayer book."

Socialist, socialism • Person or philosophy that believes individuals should control the economy and use its resources equally and fairly for all people; a major political movement in the twentieth century.

Sodom • Biblical city (Genesis 18:16–19:28) that was destroyed by God because of the evil behavior of its residents.

Solel Boneh • Arm of Israel's labor movement (Histadrut) that concentrates on building, industry, public works, and economic development.

Southern Lebanese Army • Military force friendly to Israel that patrolled the border between **Lebanon** and Israel.

Soviet Union • A federation of seventeen Soviet Socialist Republics that came into being in the 1920s after the Communist Revolution and continued until its breakup in 1998.

SS *(Schutzstaffel)* • Division of the **Nazi** army intensely loyal to **Hitler** that was responsible for the majority of Jewish deaths during the *Shoah*.

Stalin, Josef (1879–1953) • Ruler of the **Soviet Union**, hostile to Jews and **Zionism**.

sub-Saharan Africa • Approximately one-third of the African continent is composed of the **Sahara Desert**, which runs from east to west in the middle of the continent. Sub-Saharan Africa refers to the part of the continent south of this huge desert.

Tanach • Hebrew, "the Bible." The word is composed of the first letter of the names of the three sections of the Bible: Torah, *N'vi-im* (Prophets), and *K'tuvim* (Writings).

Technion • A technical university in **Haifa** (Israel) founded by German-Jewish immigrants in 1912. A debate occurred before classes began in 1924 about whether the language of teaching would be German or Hebrew; Hebrew won!

tel • Earthen mound where ancient ruins are found by archaeologists.

Temple Mount • Large hill in the center of **Jerusalem** where both **King Solomon**'s Temple and the **Second Temple** were built. Now location of the **Dome of the Rock** and the **Al-Aqsa Mosque**.

tzedakah • Hebrew, "righteousness, justice"; usually used to mean charity.

tzofim • Hebrew, "Israeli youth scouts."

ulpan • Intensive Hebrew language course.

United Nations International Refugee Organization • Arm of the United Nations responsible for the human needs and resettlement of refugees.

War of Independence • When Israel became independent on May 14, 1948, its Arab neighbors attacked the new state in an effort to prevent it from remaining in existence. Israel won.

West Bank • Area north of **Jerusalem** and **Jericho** along the **Jordan River** that was captured by Israel in 1967 and may today become the core of a Palestinian state.

Weizmann Institute of Science • Science research institute in Rehovot (Israel) founded in 1949.

Yad Vashem • Memorial and museum in **Jerusalem** to the Holocaust/*Shoah* and its victims.

Yadin, Yigael (1917–1984) • Israeli military leader and archaeologist, well-known for his work deciphering the Dead Sea Scrolls and excavating Masada.

yahrzeit • Yiddish, "anniversary of a loved one's death."

Yahel • A **kibbutz** related to the **Israel Movement for Progressive Judaism** located in the **Arava** region, south of the **Dead Sea**.

yeshivah (plural: yeshivot) • Hebrew, "school for advanced Jewish learning."

Yiddish • Language used in daily conversation by Jews in Eastern Europe before World War II; composed of German, Hebrew, and Slavic elements.

yishuv • Jewish community in Palestine before 1948.

Yom Kippur • Second of Judaism's **High Holy Days**, the Day of Atonement.

Yom Kippur War • Attack by **Egypt** and **Syria** on October 6, 1973, which was **Yom Kippur**. It lasted nearly three weeks and ended in Israeli victory.

y'ridah • Hebrew term for the act of leaving Israel to live elsewhere.

Zechariah • Biblical **prophet** who wrote after the Jews returned from Babylonian exile in 538 B.C.E.

Zion (Zionism) • Israel or the Promised Land, centering on **Jerusalem** (and the philosophy that Jews should establish and support a Jewish homeland in Zion).

Zionist • Someone who believes in **Zionism**.

Zohar • "The Book of Splendor"; the major work of Jewish mysticism or **Kabbalah**, written by Moses de Leon in southern France about 1245 C.E.